I0671704

The King David Syndrome

Ormine Thompson

Published by Oogoobe Tree Publishers, 2026.

The King David Syndrome
Copyright © 2018 by Ormine Thompson
All rights reserved. No part of this book may be reproduced in any form or by any electronic or mechanical means including information storage and retrieval systems, without permission in writing from the author. The only exception is by a reviewer, who may quote short excerpts in a review.

This book is a work of fiction. Names, characters, places, and incidents either are the products of the author's imagination or are used fictitiously. Any resemblance to actual persons, living or dead, events, or locales is entirely coincidental.

Ormine Thompson

This is a work of fiction. Similarities to real people, places, or events are entirely coincidental.

THE KING DAVID SYNDROME

First edition. January 20, 2026.

Copyright © 2026 Ormine Thompson.

ISBN: 978-1732880337

Written by Ormine Thompson.

Table of Contents

Glass-building gods and mass-media saints connived with pestilence and sledgehammered our doors to invade our rooms.

Ormine Thompson

aswainsen@yahoo.com
Oogoobe Tree Publishing

Glass-building gods and mass-media saints connived with pestilence and
sledgehammered our doors to invade our rooms.

Ormine Thompson

The King David Syndrome

Chapter 1

It was a typical warm, tranquil February day in the Florida woods. A breeze tickled the thick canopy of pine, oak, and other hardwood trees in a glen. Sunbeams muscled through the foliage like angled beams of liquid light, and butterflies frolicked on the new growth on the ground. A flock of birds cawed and soared across the blue sky. A mockingbird piped a note in reply.

Minute particles traversed the light beams back and forth like jewel beads on their way up to infinity's park. A woodpecker shattered the silence high on a dead trunk.

Two squirrels raced up a giant oak in fright, zipped on a limb, leaped to another branch, and disappeared into the forest. Rats bolted into holes under a massive pine root as the woodpecker lifted its hammer, held it, listened, and flew away. Nearby birds took to the sky and chattered their protests at the yet-unseen disturber's intrusion.

A motor roared, and an army-camouflaged pickup truck pulled up between two trees.

The painted-face male driver in military fatigues reclined the driver's seat, drew a baseball cap over his face, and folded iron-hard, sun-blasted arms across his chest, a gigantic unlit Cuban cigar in his mouth.

An M24 rifle rested on his lap, and a pistol fitted with a silencer lay beside an expensive electronic recording device. A playful child had scratched an arrow through a heart on the red recorder's cover as an act of love. The wind blew the dog tags, hung by a silver chain, on the gearshift through the open windows.

Male laughter and a small object splashing in water emitted from the device's speaker, and two males conversed over the sound of the wind. The excellent reception sounded as if the men were standing or sitting close to the transmitter bugs.

The sniper stretched a firm hand and pressed the recorder button, his face concealed.

"JW, please, bring my shades?"

"Okay, Dad."

Mr. Sniper's hand darted and pointed his pistol out the window as a giant bush rat emerged from a trash-filled hole. The animal stood on its hind legs and gazed into the gun's barrel at the mouth of its lair.

He squeezed the trigger; the rodent dashed into the cavity, and the bullet kicked up trash in the spot the rodent vacated.

"Motherfucker, we're not in St. Petersburg."

He hated rats since they mauled him in a gutter one wintry night as he hid from the FSB years ago in St. Petersburg's slums. Four involuntary twitches ran through his right leg, where the rodents had gnawed the muscles.

"We've enough critters in America. Why did Russian stinkers eat me alive?"

He chuckled.

"My wife said it was because I lay with them."

He fired three more bullets into the hole and refolded his arms, the gun in his hand.

At the western edges of the forest, a broad man-made lake shimmered on private property up to the tree line. A hardwood jetty faced an upscale wood cabin. Pines, oaks, and an extensive patch of tropical mahogany forest surrounded the four corners of the lake. An unpaved road cut through scattered growth to an open metal gate with a chain and padlock hanging from it.

JW Dawes, a tall, athletic, girls-crazy, handsome twenty-year-old clad in high-end outdoor gear, fished on one end of the pier with Mr. Dawes, his Father.

The pen of time drew hard lines in Mr. Dawes' face and left sixty-year-old tracks, but skipped his cunning, bright eyes. Mr. Dawes' prideful eyes sparkled at JW like a hungry hunter who eyed a careless deer as it wandered up the trail.

Mr. Dawes hung his light windbreaker on a post and flicked his Rolex off his lower wrist; his son wore an identical one. The watch swung like his arms had lost weight, and the band needed adjustment. The sunlight glistened off the water as he cast his line. The elder Dawes imported Walleye Pike, Trout, Bluegill, Largemouth Bass, Paiche from Peru, Bocachico fishes from Colombia, and ten species of crawfish for his private lake fed by an underground river.

An expensive custom truck parked in the driveway reflected rays like a lighthouse beacon. Mr. Dawes flicked his rod and glanced at JW's sturdy six-foot frame.

He marveled for the millionth time at how the boy robbed his mother of her delicate, pleasing lines and employed them to mask his father's rough patches.

"Dad, we've lost some brave, exemplary people on the Columbia Shuttle yesterday."

"A sad day in our country's history, indeed."

"Do you think NASA's negligence?" JW asked.

"Let's not jump to conclusions too soon, and I've instructed the office to set up a ten-million memorial fund for the families in your name," Mr. Dawes said.

"Why me and not you?" JW asked.

"Give me a minute. How're you and Regina?"

"We're doing excellent."

"Regina is not a girlfriend-type gal," Mr. Dawes said.

JW's head shot up from his baits.

"Dad."

"Slow down, boy. Regina's wife material."

JW pumped a fist.

"Throughout history, many eminent men have made the mistake of marrying a born mistress and kept a natural-created wife for a side-woman," Mr. Dawes said.

A fish reared and splashed back in the water.

"Son, that's the greatest mistake a man can ever make, and in some cases, it's a fatal one, too," Mr. Dawes continued.

"I loved Regina with all my heart and soul."

"Please tell me you nailed her."

JW grinned at Mr. Dawes; he slapped him on his shoulder and winked. Mr. Dawes rubbed his nostrils from the pungent outdoor aromatic therapy.

"I want you to marry her. She possesses the foundation successful men build upon. She owns it all: beauty, self-assurance, smarts, and virtue."

"Thanks, Dad."

Mr. Dawes held his hand for a high-five, and JW reciprocated.

"After the marriage comes the fun," Mr. Dawes said.

JW's quizzical, water-colored eyes drilled into his father's.

"You refer to what they call cheating, don't you?" JW asked.

"We shortchanged the IRS and the occasional business associates as Alpha dogs at opportune times. Like my father before me, we owned significant wealth and an insatiable appetite for innovative, hot women. Son, we're masters of King David's Syndrome."

Mr. Dawes reeled in his line and lost a bite. JW rebaited his hook and cast it back out.

"The game of life laid the rules at every stratum. Your mistress should not come—"

Mr. Dawes pulled at another nibble.

"Close to your foundation and your home. The two must never mingle lest you're forced to crush the offender," Mr. Dawes continued.

Mr. Dawes chopped a vicious arm down, and JW nodded in agreement.

"Son, a successful man never crushes his home. Today, all I own is yours—my assets and my secrets."

JW smiled, and his eyes roved the lake, taken aback by his Father's sudden generosity. Nevertheless, he couldn't hide the admiration and the fantastic array of pleasurable things he planned to ride forward like a celestial chariot.

Why would his father retire at sixty? He glanced at the older man's profile and the firm jawline, the cheekbone more prominent than he remembered.

Unknown to JW, doctors had placed a five-year stamp on Mr. Dawes' life four years ago.

Mr. Dawes smiled at JW, and the boy failed to read the messages in his eyes.

He kept his secret from his family to avoid them pampering him and the ceaseless worry about him. Influential men killed when it was prudent to and embraced their demise like lovers when it arrived. They don't hide in crevices smothered by dread of imminent doom or suffocated in pain under the limbs of those who loved them. Fate rivaled death by an exhaustive margin. The silent killer spread inside his body like weeds in a flower garden. Close to his bedridden stage, he would check into an Oregon physician-assisted suicide clinic, a damn state he always loved.

Mr. Dawes puffed his right arm muscle.

Who to tell? Innovative medicine might keep his body together for another five years.

A car pulled up before the cabin. Two beautiful, high-energy, half-naked young women, cheery and filled with life, raced from the vehicle. Lidia squealed in delight.

"There go the fishes to the far end of the lake," JW said.

"These girls don't sing Regina's or your mother's songs. Come, the fish are on their day off. Throw them the baits. We've fun to live."

JW maximized his new billionaire's smile as if he wanted to outdo the sunlight, mindless of future harbingers as they lurked between warm days and calm nights disguised as fate and karma.

Chapter 2

Illisya Haynes stood in the concrete shed's open doorway, in her backyard, and held on to the metal door. She exuded a princess's aura of beautiful things to come, although her attire reeked of the lower-middle-class from her head to her feet.

Mr. Haynes faced the wall and placed lifelike human-skin masks on mannequin heads on the shelf. Heavy weapons, knives, swords, and spy gadgets lined the walls of the windowless shed.

Playing children's laughter from vaulted the new eight-foot wall around the typical concrete ranch-type house painted white at the eastern end of NW 175 Street. Rotten ackee and avocados carpeted the lawn from two trees in the backyard. One or more ackee trees in the back of a South Florida home indicated that Jamaicans once occupied the property.

Illisya's so-called best friend, Kali Falkner, lived south in Coral Gables, a different world from hers. Mr. Haynes, worked for Mr. Falkner, and the dynamics between the haves and the have-nots tolerated the unequal friendship.

She glanced at the mess and remembered how he promised to cut down the trees four years ago when they moved onto the property. Each tree grew taller and dumped a zillion more fruits on the lawn daily.

Mr. Seymore, a short, round-faced Jamaican man, bought ackee from Mr. Haynes for his Curry Kitchen restaurant in the 183rd Street Flea Market Plaza. Last year, he sold the place, moved to Fort Lauderdale, and the fruits rotted on the ground.

Please show me a slim restaurant owner, somebody.

She opened her mouth to ask, but Bill next door hammered something metallic. Whatever he beat sounded like a wayward bell.

"What is Billy Boy breaking?" Illisya asked.

The roof of the next-door house rose a yard over their high concrete barrier.

Illisya gawked at Mr. Hayne's broad back.

"Dad, when will you teach me how to make and wear disguises?"

Mr. Haynes answered without turning.

"Illisya, you're twelve. Why the rush?"

"Does time sit on fences and wait for little soon-to-be thirteen-year-old girls?"

Mr. Haynes chuckled.

"I guess I'll have to dash back to you soon," he said.

"I want to make a mask of little rich, dopey Kali Falkner and land her in trouble at school. So, will you please expedite your return?" Illisya asked.

"Her old man paid for your schooling."

"I'm not after her father, though," Illisya said.

Mr. Haynes laughed and bent over, and Illisya spotted him on the shoulder.

"Where did you catch those ugly fishes you brought home today?" Illisya asked.

"They're called Paiche, and they came from Peru. You can only snag them in one private lake in America."

"Do you own a private lake?"

"Are you a comic?"

"I'm off to Meg's house, and two of the uglies from your private lake are hers," Illisya said.

"What do you see in the old freak?"

"She's an assertive woman and my mom's best friend. You're not a racist, Dad, so you dislike her because she refused to sleep with you."

"That's the spirit, Illisya. When it doesn't rain, it's a dry spell."

Illisya giggled as she skipped away toward the house's rear door. Mr. Haynes shook his head as the old dilemmatic questions rushed him.

Where do her wits and savvy come from? Not from her mom, the teacher, or me, the killer.

Based on his background, he figured he may have to slay a mountain to keep the CIA and NSA's hands off her. Without a doubt, the various agencies had already compiled files on her based on the father-daughter angle. Nevertheless, she would not waste half her life on pennies and betrayal.

If she took on the trade, it would be as an independent contractor, and if anyone approached her behind his back...

He flicked his wrist and buried his knife blade into a mannequin's torso to the hilt.

Chapter 3

Four months later, Illisya celebrated her thirteenth birthday on Mr. Falkner's twenty-five-million-dollar yacht, courtesy of Mr. Falkner's generosity. Kali, Bill from next door, and twenty-five of Kali's wealthy friends mingled on deck. A month separated the ages of Kali, Bill, and Illisya. Kali took Bill's hand, hauled him amongst the dancers, and gazed down at Illisya in the boat's cockpit. Kali danced on Bill, moved on, and left him in no man's land looking silly. She strutted across the deck, imitating the British Royals' mannerisms, and enthralled her peers. She whirled from bow to stern as if she ran Illisya's party. Illisya monitored Kali's actions from the wheelhouse, standing beside the Captain, and couldn't care less about the fun and games. The Captain would give her the wheel when they cruised through the Government Cut as part of her present, and Kali would pay another day.

"Look at her, she hijacked Bill and everyone else's attention. I'm not mad, but I didn't ask her to be my hostess or try to steal her friends at her celebrations."

Captain Zebby caught the play between the two girls, and as a have-not himself, he rooted for Illisya's team.

Mr. Haynes and Mr. Falkner conversed at the far bulkhead, sipping from tall glasses, their backs to the activities. Mrs. Haynes hung at the fringe of the other mothers, uncomfortable and out of place. Illisya frowned at her mother's awkwardness in the presence of the wealthy women.

She made a silent vow to the universe that she wouldn't be an awkward cow on Broadway in the company of queens, princesses, or angels at any time in her life. She caught Mr. Falkner's discreet eyes eating into her like an expensive meal and hoped her Dad rebuked the multi-millionaire about the lewd way he gawked at her. She believed it was obnoxious of him to mark her out as a grown woman he'd booked for a late supper or something.

Dad, although you work for the man, I shall soon have a conversation with you about his behavior. You two are into industrial espionage and spy-related things. I hope you don't think of underage girls inappropriately, as he did me. My skin crawled from his sneak peeks, and when I turned my back, I sensed his obscene eyes beating my butt like a log.

The vessel displaced water as it left Biscayne Bay behind.

Captain Zebby, a Jamaican man with robust arms, held the wheel and mumbled to himself as usual—a home-repair handyman by trade when not in Mr. Falkner's service. Mr. Falkner found Zebby at Rick's Café in Negril when the Captain docked a boat full of tourists from Montego Bay one day years ago. The natives at the bar argued about how Zebby sailed from the Cayman Islands to Jamaica through Hurricane Gilbert in 1988.

"Another version said they voyaged from Cuba or Grenada," a woman said.

"Cuba? We didn't have diplomatic relations with Cuba at the time," a man shouted.

"Why couldn't he wait the storm out?" Winston asked.

"The rumor said the storm ambushed them on a smugglers' run," Ruby said.

"It must have been a valuable cargo," Winston said.

"Yeah, a cargo hold filled with an African prince's gold and diamonds," Mr. Chen said.

The stories intrigued Mr. Falkner, and he accosted Zebby on the dock. They conversed for ten minutes; Zebby leaned and rocked like a boat in high wind, and his steel-like hands held an imaginary helm before him as he relayed his story. Mr. Falkner handed him his card at the end of his tale.

"Call me when you're in Miami," Mr. Falkner said.

"Yes, sir, I sure will," Zebby said.

Zebby called Mr. Falkner a week later and became his part-time Captain on shady trips in and out of tight spots for the last fifteen years.

Zebby handed the wheel to Illisya. She grasped it; a joyous scream raced from her gut, and she suppressed it. It's chilly for a Captain to scream. Zebby towered over her, and she glanced up at his rugged profile.

He sailed through the hurricane and squeezed it with his vice-grip hands.

Illisya chortled at her joke.

"Steady her as you go, mate," Zebby growled.

"Aye, aye, Captain."

▲ ▲ ▲

Hours later, Bill helped Illisya remove the last of her presents from the car trunk. Illisya slapped Bill on his sunburnt shoulder inside the house, and the boy winced.

"Ouch, Illisya, I showed you my burns."

Illisya giggled.

"Open the presents, and if you find anything boy-boyish, it's yours. I'm gonna take a shower and go straight to bed."

"Thanks, Illisya."

Bill bumped her with his sizeable heavyweight boxer's fist.

Early Saturday morning, Mr. Haynes knocked on Illisya's bedroom door.

"Wake up, Illisya, and let's finish those masks you started."

"I want to, but the morning hasn't woken yet."

"Operatives from the other side killed and stole secrets while you slept."

"Not fair. Go and hound bad people for me and tell Mom you robbed me of my night's rest."

Mrs. Haynes ambled up in her printed PJs and placed an arm on Mr. Haynes's shoulder.

"Dumped me at the bend and continued. I told you to stick with dolls and leave your father's tradecraft," Mrs. Haynes said.

"Mother, you're not helping," Illisya growled from behind the door.

The morning sun renovated South Florida six degrees shy of frying everything and everyone. The aroma of pancakes, fried bacon, and eggs watered mouths in Mrs. Haynes's kitchen. She pulled a tray from the oven. Illisya raced into the kitchen, her face covered in a hyper-realistic mask of Kali and her T-shirt splattered with silicone scraps.

"Good morning, Mrs. Haynes," Illisya said in Kali's perfect upper-class accent.

Mrs. Haynes hopped in fright. Illisya stole a pancake, laughed, and dashed for the bathroom.

Chapter 4

Mr. Haynes left for unknown destinations, and one or more of his mysterious trips lasted two or three months or more. He never told his family where he went or when to expect him back.

Illisya alighted from her school bus on a Monday afternoon and keyed herself in through the side gate. Bill missed her by a beat as his bus pulled up and drove away. He shouted from his side of the wall.

"Illisya, open the door. Let's work on the math problem."

She pushed her head through a window.

"Later, Billy Boy."

Her Mrs. Haynes worked late, teaching middle school. Illisya flung her book bag onto the living room sofa and shot through the back door. She opened the workshop door and closed it behind her.

"Billy Boy, you're not allowed in here," she said to herself.

She pulled the covers off two unfinished masks and sat around them.

▲ ▲ ▲

Two years later, the bugle sounded at Gulfstream Park Racetrack as Kali and Illisya spilled from Mr. Falkner's Bentley in the valet area. Their ears pricked like old racehorses as they raced to the trackside. Both girls touched fifteen and filled out in places where dreamers, abusers, and traffickers began to lend a serious eye. Kali beat Illisya to the rails as the horses paraded before the tote board.

"I'll take number six, the gray," Kali said.

"You can have him."

"Why are you so generous?"

"It's fifty to one," Illisya said.

"I'm sticking with him, and he's gonna run before your pick."

"Okay, I'll ride the one home. And what's the wager?" Illisya asked.

"Hey, if you win, you can keep the outfit I loaned you."

"You got a deal."

She gazed down at Kali.

"Bets on, and I, too, will acquire wealth someday unless they stop making money."

Kali grinned in her face.

Mr. Falkner leaned on the counter away from the track, and Kali ran and slapped him on the back.

"Daddy, Daddy, we're over here."

JW and Regina Dawes rooted for their horses in the glass house, as the ten-cent superfecta gamblers downstairs called it. Regina impressed the Sunday afternoon crowd in a sky-blue two-piece combo. JW flew under the radar in a starched white shirt under a powder-blue blazer, jeans, and loafers.

JW's high school friend's father raced two horses, and the buddies assembled in the horsemen's saloon. They dunked shots, whooped, and laughed like the owners of the moment. Jean, the floor sweeper was a former Haitian Secret Police officer, and he blended into his job as an unnoticeable man. His cunning broom swept on the tails of wealthy punters, and he tracked the young, inexperienced group and their handful of betting vouchers.

The affluent young hoodlums staggered from the bar to the betting counter. Jean swept tickets and lurked behind the young guns as they made huge wagers on Kali's long-odds pick. The bunch stumbled back to the bank of monitors, and Jean followed like an unseen shadow. To Jean, most kids couldn't tell a horse's head from its tail, much less navigate winning tickets under the influence of liquor. His dustpan and broom vibrated in his hands, ready to sweep vouchers as patrons discarded them.

Number six won the race at sixty-five to one. The group hopped, shouted, hugged, spilled drinks, and dug through their vouchers.

"Is this one a winner, JW?" a young man asked.

"I'm not sure, dude."

"They said to put a hundred across the board on it. I don't understand what it means," a girl said.

"Throw it away. The five-hundred-win ticket is the one you should concentrate on, Jen," the dumb drunk said.

Betting vouchers fell, and Jean swept them into his dustpan like a whale amid a school of herrings. Minutes later, he drifted away like a trained cloak-and-dagger operative.

"The hundred-dollar-across-the-board ticket can buy me the Toyota SUV I fancy at the use car dealers, no more bus rides for me."

▲ ▲ ▲

JW left the University of Miami and took his Business, Math, Economics, and Social Studies professors' home at three times their regular salaries. In the second year, he threw in an anthropologist who stole or borrowed Indiana Jones' hat.

JW and the virtuous damsel Regina married five months before his twenty-first birthday and bought a mansion on Fisher Island. Naturopathic and mainstream medicines kept Mr. Dawes an active man for five more years. JW lived by his Feather's mantra and pursued the King David Syndrome without qualms. As a rule, he reached home by 7:00 p.m., regardless of what secret shenanigans he and his father indulged in during his waning days. The rock-hard law of their creed to never rock the home base, or their foundation stood as the anchor of their existence.

Regina earned a degree in Early Childhood Education and History from Florida State University. She never applied her skills in a full-time classroom, except for voluntary work after her marriage. The joke at her parents' dining table before the billionaire liaison went something like this: We delivered them, healed the sick, and you taught them.

Regina owned an introverted soul and didn't care much for the high-octane social gangs of Miami, unlike her husband, who did regular business sorties. After the birth of her daughter, Regina became a more traditional housewife. She nurtured Mary at home until they decided she should mingle with other children and learn social skills independently. Her husband put no pressure on her, and Mrs. Regina Dawes enjoyed a happy marriage.

▲ ▲ ▲

Illisya once said, "Time doesn't sit and wait for little girls." Two weeks before her sixteenth birthday, Illisya and Mr. Haynes practiced martial arts at Virginia Key Beach on a cloudy, ugly day. The wind blew off the water and buffered the stench from the nearby sewer plant.

Mr. Haynes attacked Illisya with kill strikes and backed her into knee deep water. Illisya swept her right foot, splashed water in his face, unleashed flurries of kill punches, and forced him ten yards up the sand.

They trained for a good hour and cooled down on a fallen sycamore log. Illisya fished a cold jug of water from the Igloo. From behind, they sat close together like lovers to the casual observer.

"So, all these years, you harbored an apprehension of water?" Mr. Haynes asked.

"Are you saying I should've let you drown me?"

"Who taught you Krav Maga, the shoulder bump, and the knuckles-to-the-windpipe techniques?"

YouTube videos. I worked on it for months. Mr. Dawes is gonna jump me. His intentions lit up his eyes like a neon sign," Illisya said.

"I would destroy him."

"Suppose his lust overcame his concerns?"

"You have the skill to neutralize any threat and don't hesitate a second to utilize your death strike. Second chances are rare in mortal combats."

Illisya guzzled water and bounced his shoulder in affirmation.

▲ ▲ ▲

Kali's seventeenth birthday came around in just under two weeks, and Illisya's Earth Strong, as she called hers, came up a couple of days later. People borrowed the slang from hip Island kids at school, who credited the moniker to Jamaica's Rastafarians.

Maybe they didn't coin the term, but it's dope.

On a business-like Monday, Illisya searched from one end of the campus to the other.

"Kali, where are you?" she shouted into her phone.

"Zoey, have you seen Kali?"

"I saw her in the hall after the first bell."

Illisya sat in the gym and called Kali's phone ten times without getting an answer.

"Did you find her?" Chad asked.

"No. I don't want to inform her parents and cause trouble."

"I'll ask around."

"Okay, Chad. I'm lost."

Perturbed, Illisya waited under a poinciana tree away from the mad-dash after-school rush, and a dark-windowed Toyota Camry pulled up. The driver's window rolled halfway down, and Mr. Falkner called:

"Over here, Illisya. Get in the car."

Her heart almost broke her ribs and queried: Oh no, something terrible befell Kali. Why is Mr. Falkner driving incognito in a common man's car?

Mr. Falkner smiled as she slid into the vehicle, and his intentions glinted in the corners of his eyes, but in her perturbed state, she dismissed the meaning of that strange glint.

"Is Kali okay, sir? I searched for her all day."

"She sneaked away to a bash rehearsal on my yacht. I thought she told you to play hooky and couldn't find you. I told her it would be better if y'all kept one gigantic seventeenth-birthday shindig together. Yes, it shocked me too when she agreed and sent me to fetch you."

"So, whose car are you driving?"

"One of the helpers. I didn't want to create a scene in my Bentley," Mr. Falkner said.

"Let's go crash something, Mr. Falkner."

Mr. Falkner docked his dinghy in the scent of the Virginia Key sewer plant, and the yacht bobbed on the water hundreds of yards out in the passage. Excitement stole Illisya's sense of observation as the dinghy drew close, and she overlooked the empty deck.

"I bet Kali and her friends hid in the cabins to surprise you. However, the joke will be on them," Mr. Falkner said.

"Typical Kali, sir."

"Change into one of the new swimsuits, lift anchor, and head for open water. I'm gonna round up Kali and her critters," he said.

A pleased Illisya gunned the sleek vessel across the smooth bay for the ocean. She sailed five nautical miles from the Government

Cut before Mr. Falkner returned on deck, swathed in a towel, his sixty-eight-year-old tanned upper-body muscles ripped. Illisya glanced back at the western sun and the Miami skyline, and it hit her.

The bait-and-lure technique caught and isolated her in the middle of nowhere. Her introverted persona dulled her danger signal and made her comfortable at the helm. She should have detected the threat earlier and taken evasive action.

A calm Illisya rifled inside her bag for her burner phone. Mr. Haynes insisted she always carry it for emergencies during one of their intense training sessions.

On the day in question, she had swung a vicious Bo, caught her him under his arm, and he fell to his knees. She ran to his aid out of concern, and he swept her feet from under her and dumped her on her butt.

"In a situation like this in the field, you finish the assailant with your gun. You're not a doctor, don't check people's pulses."

"Yes, sir."

He trained her to be merciless, never dropping her guard, always riding on full lungs of oxygen. Yet in her glee, she fell for a pedophile's scam.

"Lower your anchor and come here, Illisya."

"Where's everyone else, sir?"

"Rid yourself of the formalities, will you, and call me Rodzik."

He popped a champagne bottle, filled two flutes, and opened a jar of Royal Osetra caviar—Illisya's favorite indulgence when she rode the yacht. Her body tensed to steel as she stumbled toward Rodzik in sly, shy aggressiveness.

Rodzik handed her a flute, and she took a secret fighting stance.

"I'm underage."

"Come on, you've always wanted to be alone with me. I've seen it in your eyes."

Illisya smiled and intensified the fire in Rodzik's eyes.

How many ways should I kill this child-molester fool if he touches me?

"I want to go home," Illisya said.

"Come to me, you ungrateful little bitch. I've paid thousands for your school tuition over the years. Free rides are a scarce commodity in life, young miss."

He lunged for her arm, and she danced away. The towel around his waist fell on the deck. Illisya feigned horror and backed up against the bulkhead. Falkner rushed her. She slammed her shoulder into Rodzik's and knocked him off balance. He stumbled, marveling at her upper-body strength. Her arm darted like a cobra for his windpipe; her knuckles struck and crushed his trachea.

Mr. Falkner's eyes widened, and it took his oxygen-deprived brain forever to comprehend his dilemma. His knees buckled onto the deck; he made horrible sounds, and a feeble hand clawed at his throat.

Illisya spooned a mouthful of caviar and ate as Mr. Falkner died in his urine.

She waited ten minutes and called.

"Hello."

"Dad, where are you? I heard you borrowed a boat and sped somewhere beyond the Government Cut."

"I can't believe the mouth on your mother."

"My sleeping arrangements over here didn't work out. Can you follow my ping?"

"Keep your lights on and catch a snapper or two."

"Sure, Daddy."

She guzzled water and quenched her dragon's breath.

Mr. Haynes boarded the yacht in the dark while Illisya wiped her presence off everything she touched. He peeled back the covers and peeked at his part-time boss's body on the dark deck.

"Did you swab?"

"I sure did."

"Do you want us to go over it again?"

"It couldn't hurt."

The vessel coasted five leagues away from where Mr. Haynes found it, and he encased the body in chains and readied it for burial. As usual, he hid his face and kicked Falkner's body overboard. Illisya sailed the vessel back into the bay.

Kicking a billionaire's body off his boat is not a proper burial, and I don't have to look it up. However, at times, one must improvise, Illisya mused.

They abandoned the ship, rode Mr. Haynes's small outboards to shore, and reached home at 3:16 a.m. Illisya headed for her room.

"Do you want to talk?" Mr. Haynes asked in the darkened house.

"What for, or about?" Illisya asked and locked her bedroom door behind her.

"Acid ran through her flipping veins."

"I heard that," Illisya said through the door.

At 7:00 a.m., Kali rang Illisya's phone.

"Where were you yesterday?" Illisya snapped, her edgy morning voice sharp as a razor.

"Guess where."

"Bitch, it's too early for it," Illisya snarled.

"Well, I and my mother darted over to Paris, France, on a pre-celebration shopping trip. Loosen your knots, I got you something."

"Do they have flea markets in France?"

"Am I that horrible, dearie?"

"Without redemption. And bye, I'm gonna be late for school."

She pocketed the phone.

"Who darts to a foreign country? Is she Supergirl? And don't you and your mother miss your father yet?"

▲ ▲ ▲

The midsummer sun pelted Falkner's magnificent mansion at the center of lavish, well-maintained grounds on Tahiti Beach Island Road in Coral Gables. Nine months had passed since Mr. Falkner disappeared at sea. The immaculate lawn spread outward, ringed with varieties of palms and bougainvillea lining the perimeters.

One of the four garage bays rolled open, and Mrs. Falkner covered her elegant forty-five-year-old body in a Chanel floral piece. She settled into a milk-white Bentley convertible and dared angels to read her expression. The police and the Coast Guard had searched Biscayne Bay for her husband's body for two weeks, nine months ago, without avail. Mrs. Falkner sat for five long minutes, neither pleased nor distressed, and drove down the driveway to lunch with Defarris, an affluent local politician bitten by the Washington, D.C., ambition bug.

Brainy Bill Kelly, country-robust and rugged at seventeen, dumped boxes in the garage and followed the Bentley with his eyes. He traced a finger along a Lamborghini's seam; stepped outside into the sun.

"The fervor for everyday things sits at most people's arm's length and might as well be on Mars where I'm concerned."

Bill wet his dried lips. He would hit twenty in less than three years and vowed to have at least one of his dreams solidified into a hard object.

Illisya brought Bill along whenever the Falkners needed manual labor inside their home. Bill pulled in $300 for an hour or two of work. He dreamed of money and craved Illisya, or even dopey Kali Falkner on his plate someday. On the ride down, he wondered if Kali would cry for him if he went missing; she hadn't for her father. The press's blanket coverage of Mr. Falkner's disappearance slid off her like water off a duck's back. Bill had never seen her reflective or sad over the mystery.

"Fuck, how cold is Antarctica?"

Illisya Haynes, three months shy of her eighteenth Earth day, perched on the arm of the sofa in the mansion's TV room, transfixed by the screen and surrounded by luxury. Her overwhelming beauty, however, could not disguise her continual state of resource limitation.

"On money matters, the Dawes Enterprise installed JW Dawes as the youngest CEO of a Fortune Five Hundred company at the age of twenty-five," the anchor announced.

JW's photo flashed on the screen. Illisya exhaled, covered her mouth in awe, and drifted closer to the TV, pulled as if by spell.

"Wow. Damn. I'm waiting for you. I've gotta have you," Illisya whispered.

Kali Falkner entered, draped in the troubled seventeen-year-old wealthy-girl uniform, sour, proud, and condescending to the poor. Her mind groomed her persona like a bird of paradise in courtship. She glanced from Illisya to JW's close-up on the screen with a critical eye. When the commercial hit, she stared at Illisya in a scornful, mocking stare.

"Money dances up against money. He's out of your league, out of your range, and he lives up in Saturn's rings where you're concerned," Kali said.

Illisya smiled, and it reached for Kali with malicious claws and evil intentions.

"The beauty about tomorrow it is fearless, limitless, and fucking boundless," Illisya snapped.

"A wager, if you two ever occupy space under the same sky by consent—"

"How's your memory?" Illisya snapped.

"We golden spooners only remember what we choose to."

"We've ten hundred more boxes for the charity folks to pick up. Let's go," Bill said from the doorway.

Illisya shot Kali an eye that could rust iron and tramped out behind Bill.

"One day I'm gonna remind that bitch about today's wager. Only she won't hear a word," Illisya muttered.

Fifteen minutes later, Kali rummaged through a box and pulled out two luxurious men's wristwatches.

"My mom's giving all of Dad's stuff to charity. There are goodies in there—take what you want," Kali said.

"Can I have one of those?" Bill asked.

"Take them both."

Bill beamed, sliding his large hand into one of the gold bands and inspecting it.

"If I don't get the ball scholarship, these babies will pay for my first two years of college."

Illisya winked at him.

Kali lifted a red voice recorder. Illisya's eyes went wide.

"Hey, that's my Dad's recorder. I scratched the heart on it," Illisya said.

"Your father slaved for mine doing industrial-grade bad shit," Kali said.

"Who said?" Bill asked.

"I overheard them plenty of times. They killed people too," Kali said.

"Oh yeah, that sounds like Mr. Haynes," Bill said.

"Gimme it," Illisya said.

She snatched the recorder and popped the tape out.

▲ ▲ ▲

Kali pulled up at Mr. Haynes's gate at 4:00 p.m., Illisya, and Bill exited the vehicle. Kali peeled away as if she didn't want the next minute to catch her in the neighborhood.

Bill smiled at Illisya and lugged his bag of goodies home. Illisya slid her bag through the gate.

"Mom, put this in the house for me. I'm going to Meg's."

She hurried down the Avenue, with the old recorder tucked under her arm.

Twenty minutes later, Illisya sat on an old plastic chair on Meg's run-down front porch on Northwest 180th Street and 23rd Avenue. The sun hung low on the western horizon behind the house, while she sat in shadow on the eastern side and her right flip-flop nestled into a missing tile space. Light and darkness fused, metaphorizing the difference between the mansion's neighborhood and Meg's house.

Illisya pressed play, and Mr. Dawes's voice floated from the speakers.

"JW, we're Alpha Dog, and we owned great wealth and an insatiable appetite for smart, hot women. We ran amok through maidens as Masters of King David Syndrome."

Illisya stopped and replayed the machine, again and again.

She dashed inside, returned with a Bible, flipped pages, and read while the tape looped.

"Maidens on roofs these days return intense gazes and ulterior intentions. JW Dawes, you shall be mine. Your assets and all someday," Illisya said.

She turned the cassette over and restarted it. When it finished, she held her chin and let her thoughts wander beyond the light.

She made a secret vow to marry a man her father had spied on and from whom he had poached exotic fish years ago. Illisya smiled at the strange, uncanny cuteness of it. An epiphany struck her like a rock. She stood and paced. What she had gleaned demanded a life-altering conversation with her father.

"I'm gonna be the first urban hunter-gatherer."

She gazed into the future and saw a world planted with white and red thornless roses in her garden. Illisya smirked, sat back down, kicked up her legs, and the old chair dumped her flat on her ass.

▲ ▲ ▲

Ron, at nineteen, was built like a college quarterback, strolled by Meg's hand in hand with Lacey, his beautiful nineteen-year-old girlfriend. They had been inseparable since they were sixteen.

Illisya listened to the tape for the hundredth time, shut off the machine, and waved.

"Hi, Lacey. Hi, Ron."

They waved back. Lacey kissed Ron and ran toward Illisya in the driveway.

Ron lingered, gazing over Lacey's head at Illisya as he entered his house direct across from Meg's, as if some unseen force compelled him.

"The present of your car told the tale," Illisya said.

Lacey glanced at her sun-rusted red Chevy Nova parked in front of Ron's house. Meg called the spot Lacey's garage, for Lacey worked on it right there whenever it broke down, while Ron passed tools like a nurse assisting a surgeon.

"We went up the block to say goodbye to Ron's uncle."

"You guys are serious about enlisting, huh?" Illisya asked.

"Who wouldn't be, Illisya? Don't you see what they did to our country?"

Illisya looked away, masking her boorish indifference.

What a fucking waste. When will governments stop brainwashing beautiful young people and sending them to kill other foreign-indoctrinated motherfuckers just like themselves? What a shit-twister of negativity on a dead world. I'll never participate in a shit farce for any man or country.

"What about your car?" Illisya asked.

"You can have it," Lacey said.

Illisya hugged her.

"Oh God, Lacey thank you. I needed wheels so bad."

"It needs constant patching."

"We know our way around cars."

Ron peeked through the blinds, forever drawn. Over the years, he had tried to break the habit and failed. He didn't understand why it persisted like an addiction, because he loved Lacey beyond articulated words. He sighed and stepped away as Lacey dashed up the driveway.

Boot camp next week. If she caught me peeking at Illisya, it could derail the honey train tonight.

▲ ▲ ▲

Intelligence chatter on the dark web reported that Tublic Sanovich, a terrorist with a five-million-dollar bounty on his head had been spotted in Latvia. Mr. Haynes and the freelance bounty-hunter community descended on the region. His intel led him to Engure, a village on the Gulf of Riga, where he lay low in dark dock gutters, monitoring harbor activity.

On his third night wedged into the cracks of the pier, his earpiece whispered the home-front chime.

"It's me," he said.

"Something for the bank rolled into my path," Illisya said.

"Can it wait until I'm home?"

"It sure can. But Mom—"

"What about her?"

"Wait for it."

Darkness overtook Meg's porch. Illisya leaned back on two chair legs, folded her arms, and closed her eyes, sinking into thought after the call.

From a gutter in Engure, Mr. Haynes dialed his wife, clad in a dark trench coat and an old black fedora.

"Hi, honey," Mrs. Haynes answered.

"Don't hi honey me. You cheating piece of crap."

"What? Are you crazy?"

"You better be gone by the time I get home, or I'll show you crazy. I'm dodging bullets out here for you and our daughter, and you're in and out of your lovers' beds."

"Oh my God, where is this coming from, Robert?"

"Don't play innocent. I'm going to hurt you."

He cut the call and stared at the black water, pulse surging with anticipation of a twisted future.

Mrs. Haynes collapsed onto her bed and sprang up in mortal fear.

"Help me, Jesus. My one indiscretion happened two years before Illisya's birth. I'm running, when my husband is like this, I can't reason with him. That tone froze my soul."

She rushed into Illisya's room, lost the thought, and backed out, trembling.

"He could be around the corner. I must leave now."

She shoved clothes into a suitcase.

"I'll call Illisya on the road. I can't take her. She and her father are too close. She might've said something, but why? I'm innocent."

Chapter 5

Illisya erupted from beneath the covers of a quiet, dark bedroom in Meg's house and screamed.

"JW."

She cocked her head and listened to see if Meg stirred in her room, waited, sat up in bed and swiveled her upper body, perturbed. Her soaked pajamas clung like a wet T-shirt to her buff twenty-one-year-old torso. She clicked on the bedside lamp and ogled JW's clips and plastered photos on the walls like the possessed. She traced her finger over a recent newspaper picture of JW, his wife, and their new baby.

Illisya had read the story in the papers days earlier and mentioned Regina's problematic labor to Meg. She said wealthy people gave away too much confidential information about themselves.

"Don't folks realize bad-intentioned harbingers shadow their every step?"

Illisya slipped on baggy black sweatpants and a matching top, slung a bag over her back, and tiptoed from the room at 2:00 a.m.

▲ ▲ ▲

Illisya rode a motorcycle south to the Brickell business district and pulled up on Merry Street beneath the shadows of mahogany trees. She removed her helmet, adjusted her balaclava, and hurried toward an office block. She climbed a tree, swung from a limb, and jumped into the walled compound, landing on her haunch. The wind rustled the leaves and dislodged mahogany seed pods. They struck the concrete with hollow sounds.

Professional businesses occupied the building's ground floor. Illisya picked the OB-GYN office lock and slipped inside. She turned on a PC, hacked a file, read for two minutes, and bit her lip.

▲ ▲ ▲

At 9:00 a.m. that same morning, Illisya leaned on a rake in Meg's driveway, her old sweatpants and T-shirt soaked. She pinned her phone between her shoulder and ear.

Meg Foster, a frail seventy-four-year-old, had honed a unique philosophy of life and a razor-sharp vocabulary off the grid. She sat in an old chair on the porch and smirked.

Traumatic events had robbed Meg's life of bliss, dictated her cycles of existence, and left her mien dreary. Bitterness etched permanent mental lines, and an acidic touch settled around her once-beautiful mouth and eyes. As a child, Illisya claimed Meg's face hurt her whenever she smiled. Meg had taught school alongside Mrs. Haynes for years and missed her companionship after she disappeared. Illisya felt Meg's angst and filled the void left by her mother's departure, like a dutiful daughter.

An ambulance screamed to a stop at Ron's gate, and EMS rushed through the door. Meg joined Illisya on the lawn.

"War depleted the wheat of the Earth. I'm so happy you missed the fucking sheepie train," Meg said.

Illisya raised a hand to Meg and continued her phone conversation.

"Yes, at JW Investment they're accepting interns for the summer. Hell no, Bill. Fuck the gas station. You're too smart for it. No, I'm telling you, Billy Boy. Yes, yeah, JW Dawes. I hooked an interview for you. I said yes. Later."

Illisya hung up.

"What did you say, Lady Bitterness?" she asked.

"Shit," Meg snapped.

EMS personnel wheeled Ron into the ambulance.

"Did you know Ron carried a profound thing for you?" Meg asked.

Illisya counted on her fingers.

"Nineteen sixty-seven, seventy-seven, eighty-seven, ninety-seven. When women's virginity returns, it sure does hurt like hell. Doesn't it?" Illisya said.

Meg raised a hand as they strode into the walkway

"What do you mean? He frightened the shit out of me just now, and I don't scare, period," Illisya said.

"He went jogging this morning before you got up."

"I can take care of myself, but I don't want to run into Ron in the dead of night in Times Square."

"How uncanny. The ambulance sat over the exact spot where Lacey repaired her clunker years ago," Meg said.

Illisya was sure Lacey had told Ron about giving the car away, but it didn't matter now. The war had broken him into small, insane pieces.

Illisya had taken the Chevy home, covered it in her backyard, and never ran it on the road. Over the years, Bill asked what kind of car Mr. Haynes concealed beneath the tarp, and she told him he had left his working auto there. Bill imagined it as a muscle car, the kind bad guys and hip heroes drove in movies to gigs, and when Mr. Haynes said not to touch something, you followed orders. She fired it up once a month, and Bill wondered from his side of the wall why it never left the premises.

▲ ▲ ▲

Bill worked alone in the UM college gym, reserved for inactive players, on a hot, steamy day. He slapped his bandaged right knee in regret and replayed the freak accident in his head. *How could I blow my knee in the first season of my football scholarship?*

The quiet moments alone among the irons, away from the jocks, brought heaven to him. Evil luck followed him to the football field and wrecked his knee on a dumb play. The same knees he needed to lift Illisya into his arms and help her sort through his future NFL millions. Bill slapped his forehead a few times in remorse.

His desire to get rich enough to stand a chance with Illisya dimmed. He saw her as too intelligent to be a mere forty-niner gold miner. Anthropologists would define her more as a schematic, diabolical dagger than a digger. He loved her before he understood the word's meaning, and he still did, though she played ball on a lofty field near a five-moon planet far above his pay grade.

Bill bowed his head.

Illisya sauntered toward him unseen, hovered, giggled, and flashed him a mischievous eye.

Fallen angels visited heaven, too, and the Bible mentioned how diabolical angels plied their wares.

"So, Billy Boy, you're gonna be crunching numbers at JW Investment all summer," Illisya said.

"Are you serious?"

"You're not much on the eyes, but they loved your brain, Billy Boy."

Bill beamed.

"So, what are you gonna do?" Bill asked.

"Wouldn't you like to be in there?"

Illisya jogged away, stopped, let her shorts drop around her ankles, and bent her naked butt toward him.

"Billy Boy."

Bill glanced at her nude ass, speechless. She pulled her shorts up, giggled, and ran through the door. He licked his dry lips. His heartbeat raced, his arms weakened, and the dumbbells felt like ten tons in his hands. He lay back on the machine, closed his eyes, and conjured Illisya into beautiful scenes on the powdery white sands of a faraway beach. The beds of red flowers he carried her to in his mind quickened his breath through his teeth.

Chapter 6

Kali and her friends enjoyed a hearty lunch at Rose, a crowded South Beach café and hip folks' hangout. Among the carefree, well-off party crowd, Kali guffawed long and loud and drew the eyes of Jack O'Spade, a serial rapist and murderer on the hunt. Jack O'Spade specialized in proud, arrogant souls whose spirits he could trample, and in his eyes, Kali fit the mold.

Jack O'Spade's mother named him Ezekiel Callaghan on the day he was born. Ezekiel grew up in an ultra-conservative religious environment in Pahokee, Florida. Evolution played a role in his development, rendering him unnoticeable in a crowd, a trait ideal for stalkers and hunters.

Jack was the type of person eyewitnesses struggled to pin down after an awful incident. They offered authorities vague answers such as:

"A guy stood over there for a minute."

"What guy?"

"The dude at the counter."

"Can you describe him?"

"I don't know. He loitered by the window for a minute."

Ezekiel's voice stood out as his only distinction. It sounded like melodic bass notes strummed on instruments from Heaven by celestial beings. One of his victims once told the police:

"He wore a mask, but his voice sounded like thunder ripping velvet tablecloths on a clothesline."

The rapist-murderer maintained his freedom by mastering the most natural camouflage: being born ordinary and existing as an everyday man. His reprehensible vocation, rape and sometimes murder, continued beneath the umbrella of obscurity for seventeen years.

So, did evolution make me a chameleon man? Jack O'Spade once asked himself, and not out of regret. To Jack, his actions shouted from a pedestal to what he deemed the inferior minds of an evil world. He spoke a minimum of words to his victims for fear they would identify him by his unnatural voice.

Ezekiel raped his first victim at eighteen on his way home from church one Sunday afternoon. She was a stranger, and he did no further harm to her. The second woman he attacked scratched deep wounds into his arms. He murdered her and cut off her hands.

He considered it a mortal sin to cut off her hands and leave her alive, a fate he claimed he would not wish on a liberal demon from Congress. He convinced himself of this moral justification from the pulpit of his own warped beliefs. By the age of thirty-five, Jack O'Spade had murdered six women and raped fifty-two. He married at twenty, fathered two beautiful daughters, and never allowed family life to interfere with his alter ego. He used the moniker Jack O'Spade when communicating with victims. He presented himself to the world as Mr. Ezekiel Callaghan, a top financial advisor and CEO of his business on SW 9th Street in chic Bal Harbor.

Jack O'Spade sat at a window table, chewing on a fresh salad and whole-nut breadsticks. Kali sat four tables away from the man who had marked her as his next victim and would not have recalled him if asked minutes later.

Jack followed Kali from the café to the Falkner's Group of Companies in Brickell. He waited in the parking lot of the building she entered until he was sure she worked there. He drove away and returned at 5:05 p.m.

Jack munched on a fresh bag of mixed nuts in his car. Kali emerged from the building at 6:18 p.m., and he followed her car for two blocks before going his own way.

On the second evening, she left an hour later, and he trailed her to her apartment. On the third evening, she exited at 8:01 p.m., and Jack slapped his steering wheel, annoyed at her tardiness. He seethed as her taillights disappeared from the parking lot and waited fifteen minutes before driving home.

Precision stalkers like Jack hated people with unpredictable schedules. They preferred prey who behaved like clockwork, not like the wind, coming and going as they pleased. Jack never invested time in investigating his targets. Otherwise, he would have discovered that Kali's mother owned the companies and that his mark was an heiress.

On the fifth day of the second week, Jack O'Spade pulled an everyday panel van next to Kali's car at 5:20 p.m. The parking lot thinned within fifteen minutes to eight scattered vehicles, and he waited. Jack pulled on a pair of black gloves, folded the labels, tucked them into a trash bag, stretched out his arms, gazed down their length, and inhaled the scent of the new leather.

▲ ▲ ▲

Kali's heels clacked along the lit corridor beside the first of three enormous round columns spaced ten paces apart. She hurried into the parking lot, slowed, listened, and turned her head.

A door slammed.

She angled toward her car, stopped six yards short, listened again, sniffed the air, and moved forward.

"That's strong cologne riding the wind. Expensive, but overused."

Jack O'Spade burst from behind the van wearing a surgical mask.

A gloved hand crushed her mouth. A gun pressed hard into her back, stealing her breath.

"You can ruin your life by screaming," Jack said close to her ear, "Or by looking at my face."

He jabbed her between the shoulder blades.

"Do you understand me?"

Kali nodded, fast and shallow.

"Good," we're dancing out of here like two lovers."

He guided her forward, firm and precise. Kali walked. Her heels scraped once on the asphalt. Jack tightened his grip. She steadied. They crossed the distance without haste, a couple in step, nothing to see.

The van door slid open.

Jack turned her, lowered her head, pushed her inside and slammed the door.

▲ ▲ ▲

An hour after the kidnapping, Jack O'Spade removed a black bag from her head and blindfolded Kali on a bed in the center of a windowless, chair less room. The other pieces of furniture consisted of two fancy night tables. Kali's body shuddered, she cringed, and her head swiveled at every sound.

Jack O'Spade donned a Jack of Spades mask, locked his bank vault door, and removed Kali's blindfold.

"You can call me Jack O'Spade with an apostrophe."

"What's this place?" Kali asked.

"It's my poker room."

"I want to go home," Kali demanded.

"We haven't gambled yet."

Jack O'Spade tossed a deck of cards and two bundles of hundred-dollar bills onto the bed.

"Do you play poker?"

Kali shook her head.

"I don't want to play."

"I didn't ask if you want to play," Jack O'Spade said.

Kali nodded.

"Yes, I can play."

"Great."

Jack O'Spade undressed. Kali backed away to the far corner and gasped in horror.

"What are you doing?" Kali asked.

Her tormentor sat back on the bed.

"Whatever you win, you keep. Please undress," Jack O'Spade ordered.

Kali recoiled in shock. How can I tell this dangerous man I don't need his money and still walk out of here?

"I'm not taking off my clothes," Kali blabbered.

His steel gaze weakened her resolve further against the wall.

"I don't do dead people. Should I go and kidnap someone else for my game?"

She shook her head.

"Take your damn clothes off and sit on the bed," Jack O'Spade commanded.

"Why are you doing this to me?" Kali asked.

"I don't have the time to date and dance. I'm a busy married man and the father of two beautiful children. It's imperative I get home to them at a decent hour."

The coldness in his voice chilled Kali to the bone, and she felt her noncompliance meant her imminent demise. She thought about her honeymoon and an eager husband and stripped as if the exercise came from her head.

"Please sit in the lotus facing me and get a grip. I need the competition."

"What happens after the game?"

"We have sex, of course, and I drop you off close to wherever you wanted to go."

Kali gasped.

"It could be worse. I could have been one of those beat-you-to-a-pulp rapists or a slasher," Jack O'Spade said.

He reached for a small bag under the bed.

"I brought lubricant for my condoms, and if every woman must experience one rape, they'd have ordered my model without questions."

Kali gaped into the coldest and craziest eyes she had encountered in her short life, in total hopelessness and disgust.

Jack's eyes blazed cold fire like a religious nut who embraced centuries of entitlement narratives into every fiber of his being. Fanaticism invaded Kali's home and nudged her mother into the abyss after her father's death. The same madness confronted her across the bed. However, someone once said she who survived one day would fight in another.

"I'm not kinky. It will be plain missionary, as our Lord ordered through our pastor," Jack said.

Kali sat there and contemplated death. Who the fuck raped a woman only in missionary as his Lord ordered?

Kali and Illisya lunched at the same Rose Café where Jack O'Spade marked her a year ago. Kali aged mellow, and time taught her everyone's roses came from thorny bushes. The hard Streets acquainted her with the precise color of water and its singular purpose to fill everyone's vessels. She planned to apologize to Illisya and others for her youthful indiscretions and the disparaging remarks she had made, a discussion she left on the shelf, unaware of Illisya's angst. She plastered creamy dressing in her bowl, swallowed a mouthful of green leaves, sipped wine, and yelled,

"It's a year. I got to get away."

"Where are you going?" Illisya asked.

"We are going to Negril, Jamaica. I know you're smarter than me, but if you miss it. I meant you and I."

"Won't I be in your way?" Illisya asked.

"I could do a man in your lap. Do you realize I have animal-type sexual instinct? Yeah, it's a gift I embraced close to you know where," Kali said.

"It seems like you've got an awakening, a spinoff effect from the incident," Illisya said.

"What fucking incident? Jack violated me, and I'm not traumatized. I'm angry. I want to hurt him."

"Excuse me."

Kali opened her mouth to speak, and they both whickered instead.

Chapter 7

Kali stayed in five-star hotels worldwide, while Illisya enjoyed her first trip out of the country. She wiggled her toes in the white, powdery Negril Beach sand, which felt like warm snow between her toes. The azure sea calmed her inner demons, and she lost herself in its beauty for long, peaceful minutes. Although she grew up in Miami, South Beach never figured into her rotation. The way the warm water soothed her told her something must change as soon as possible.

The ambiance, the aroma of sunscreen lotion and alcohol, and the animal lust in the aroused residents transfixed Illisya in no woman's spot. Kali sat in a beach chair and applied a heavy layer of suntan lotion to her body. Illisya stood over her and rotated her head like a bobblehead doll.

"Gawker, could you get my back for me?" Kali asked.

Illisya lathered the sunblock onto Kali's back as two nude female swimmers raced by them and splashed water everywhere.

"To the fountain, girl. I'm parched," Kali said.

Kali took her arm, and they pushed through the crowd of half-naked bodies toward the bar.

Jack O'Spade entertained a group in loud conversation at the far end, and his voice enthralled his audience more than his story. Kali froze, and her nails bit into Illisya's arm.

"Ouch, you're hurting me."

Kali hyperventilated, and her nails dug into Illisya's arm as she pulled her away.

"What's going on, Kali?"

"Get me out of here."

"Have you seen a ghost?"

"It's him. It's him."

Illisya showed her impatience and flicked Kali's arm away.

"He who?"

"Jack O'Spade. Stinking, fucking Jack O'Spade, Illisya."

"You mean the poker player?"

"Yes, him. The one-dimensional rapist," Kali said.

"Sicko, you're saying he didn't ravage you the proper way. How do you know it's Jack?"

"I could never forget his voice. People should do shit the correct way if they're doing it."

"Are you sure it's him?"

"I'm one hundred and ten thousand percent sure."

"What do you want to do about him?" Illisya asked.

"I want the lousy fuck dead."

Illisya gawked at her.

"Kali, you couldn't kill a fly."

"I'm gonna hire someone."

"Hell no. Strangers bring trouble. If you want him dead, I'll do it," Illisya said.

"Despite what I need, you're not a nail," Kali said.

"Let's get something straight. You're doing this for the personal, unwanted ravishment and not the man's lousy job? You want me to kill him for being a degenerate, period?" Illisya asked.

"Yes. All the above, Tilly Whitelock, and you're gonna laugh at me or worse. I need a man right now," Kali said.

"Who's Tilly, and do you mean right this minute?"

Kali nodded and stomped her foot.

"All right, I believe you," Illisya said.

"Sex is therapeutic for me, and I cried with joy sometimes when a man entered me. Tilly Whitelock was a witchy demon who roamed these shores."

Illisya pointed toward Jack O'Spade, and back at Kali.

"Oh, that book you read and hauled me down here. Can you act?" Illisya asked.

"I can do anything."

"Do you think you can do him to get his guard down?"

"Yes, I can perform any role."

"Okay, you fuck him, and I'll kill him," Illisya said.

"Time is of the essence here."

"I'll take his head later. Will my timing be satisfactory, my queen?"

"I've got to have some now," Kali said.

"You go ahead. I'll hook and prep Mr. Jack O'Spade for later," Illisya said.

Kali wandered through the half-nude guests and clutched Dread, the Ganja Coordinator, a tall, skinny local man, by the backside. The guy turned and admired the barracuda hanging on her butt.

"How about it, Dread?" Kali asked.

Dread ushered her into the water. Another girl might have chosen big muscles, but Kali's experience with body size guided her toward Dread's wiry frame to fulfill her needs.

▲ ▲ ▲

The newbie and the pro re-emerged at dusk, roamed the beach, and joined a beach volleyball game. Illisya's wandering eyes indulged in discreet sightseeing on the nude beach behind her shades. They retreated under sea grape tree canopies, describing sizes, colors, razor bumps, and laughing buckets of tears. Darkness descended, and they found a cozy area under the encroaching sea grape. The fireflies' antics enthralled Illisya, and a couple ran from the insects.

"These mosquitoes have flashlights," the woman shouted.

Kali held Illisya's hand, amused, and ducked into the darkness.

"Chill and be still. They're harmless fireflies," Kali said.

"How close are nymphomaniacs and entomologists?"

"They're closer than tight-crotch virgins, I must say," Kali said. Illisya chuckled.

Hours after they arrived, Illisya found out Kali had plunged them into Stud's Town, and everyone wanted to ride. She could not walk six steps without males or females soliciting her.

"I'm parched. I need a tall Tom Collins," Kali said.

"What's that?"

"Bittersweet poison."

"I'm not drinking alcohol."

"That's why they have the ocean for people like you."

"Fuck you, bitch."

Kali placed her fingers in her mouth and whistled at a roving waitress.

"Can I have a bottle of water and a Tom Collins, please?"

"I'll be right back."

By midnight, sex, weed, and liquor drained the hedonistic guests' energy levels below zero. Kali waited in semi-darkness under the sea grape trees and hoped Jack O'Spade would save something and keep their date.

Illisya ogled the silver molten orb over the water as if she expected sharks to ascend and nip a chunk of cheese off it.

Kali knelt in the dark, her back to the distant bar.

"The confusing aroma around here smells like cosmic dust."

"Or old sex," Illisya said.

She tilted her head into the ferment for a long minute.

Waves pulsed to the heavy bass music for the few lazy dancers in the torchlight and moonlight at the bar.

Jack O'Spade meandered toward Illisya and Kali at the far end of the secluded, prearranged corner. Trees ran along a fence separating properties. Illisya strained her eyes to identify him as he marched toward them.

"Someone's coming," Illisya said.

"Is it him?"

Kali knelt with her back to Illisya, deep in the gloom.

"I'll tell you in a minute."

Illisya wandered out topless into the silver light as if bewitched.

"I see why vampires and werewolves gyrated to the moon's power. It's mesmerizing."

"So, is it him?"

"Yeah, I think it's him," Illisya said.

"I'm nervous. I'm scared and as hot as a volcano about to erupt."

"You're the sickest soul to walk the earth."

"I seriously doubt your assertions. What about you?" Kali asked.

"Shush."

Jack O'Spade approached with his lower half wrapped in a towel.

"Someone said you ran to the airport," Illisya said.

"Are you kidding? I don't usually roll like this, though," Jack said.

His voice rattled like sensual, powered thunder during intercourse.

"How do you ball on the road?" Illisya asked.

Jack O'Spade peeked at Kali's nude posterior, camouflaged by light through breaks in the foliage.

"I carry a reputation of indulgence. I'm a diverse, across-the-table alpha poker man."

"Jack, you placed a refreshed spin on honesty," Illisya said.

"It's a cushy nest you found under here," Jack said.

"Yeah, it couldn't be better."

Jack O'Spade pointed at Kali.

"Is she a shy one?"

"She's getting married next month, as I told you, and her in-laws are all over her business end. She needs a second-opinion notch on it."

"What do you mean?" Jack asked.

"Her husband-to-be would not think of anything but the old missionary style on religious grounds. She wanted to experience something else before she's all tied up," Illisya said.

Jack O'Spade chuckled.

"We're distant from holy things on these islands. Everything is different here, and I have my carving knife," Jack said.

"Where is it?" Illisya asked.

"Grab yourself a handful," Jack said.

Illisya embraced Jack O'Spade behind the neck and groped under his towel. Jack O'Spade kissed her long and hard.

"Muumuu, muumuu. Bad boys don't trample desserts ahead of the main course."

Illisya backed up to Kali, pulling Jack O'Spade along. Moments later, he took Kali from behind like a raging animal.

Illisya watched as Kali screamed and moaned, inducing Jack O'Spade. She lifted a sharpened white machete, and it reflected moonlight high above her head.

"Jack O'Spade," Illisya shouted.

Jack O'Spade turned. Illisya swung and beheaded him. Kali jumped to her feet, incensed.

"Bitch, couldn't you wait? I didn't come," Kali said.

"Sorry. What was the damn screaming about?" Illisya asked.

"Inducement. Do you know what? Pick up some first-hand experiences for yourself," Kali snapped.

"Oh yes. I'll work on it as soon as we drag the gambler and his severed head out to sea."

"I'll carry the head," Kali said.

Jack's manhood stood rock hard.

"I registered you for the torso."

"Fuck you, killer child," Kali said.

"Oh, so said the cheap whore."

They covered their mouths and stifled laughter.

Two days after the execution, Illisya and Kali sat on a log and painted insect repellent on their bodies beside Dread's car at the foot of a mountain. Dread and Kali became inseparable after their tryst in the ocean, and he invited them to his Ganja farm.

"Dread, we are finished applying the repellent," Illisya said.

"I'm waiting on my tool."

Kali gazed at the trail and wished she hadn't left the hotel compound.

An older Rasta man came down the track, handed Dread an AR-15 rifle, and slunk away onto a secondary trail without introducing himself to the girls. Kali couldn't care less, and Illisya never asked a question. Dread swung the weapon over his shoulder, and they climbed a steep trail around overhanging rocks and singing birds. The footpath leveled off, and they took a side trail downward. Fifteen minutes later, they reached the three-acre weed farm hacked from a glen. Golden buds and gum-like pistils reflected sunrays, and the aroma rose like a broken vat at a distillery.

Passion glowed in Kali's eyes as she and Dread burned their first pipe under a tree beside a wooden hut. Illisya rose, explored the farm alone, and ran into heads of corn, okra, tomatoes, eggplants, and callaloo.

"The weirdo smoked every fat golden bud she saw, and Dread took her against every fucking rock in the field."

Illisya climbed a white rock, imitated a scarecrow in the center of the field, inhaled the aroma, and mapped her ongoing operation in her head. Two intoxicated yellow-chested, black-winged birds perched on her arm, sang like drunks, and dug claws into her flesh.

"They're gonna pick your eyes out, Illisya," Kali shouted.

She twitched her arm, and the birds fluttered away. They trekked back to the hut.

"How many times did you do it?"

"It should have been more," Kali giggled.

Kali embraced Dread, and Illisya pointed to a bed made from weed buds under an overhanging rock.

"You see why I don't smoke now," Illisya said.

On the way home, the girls waited in the cool car and chitchatted for five minutes.

"What are we waiting on, Dread?"

"My armorer," he said, leaning against the car, the rifle resting against his body.

Minutes later, the old Rasta man appeared from the left, silent like a ghost. Dread handed him the gun. Illisya glimpsed disheveled hair, a gray beard, bloodshot eyes, and milk-white teeth, and the man disappeared into the bushes.

Dread drove around a corner on the narrow road home and ran into a police checkpoint. The girls grew apprehensive, and Kali grabbed Dread's leg. The police searched the car ahead of them.

"What about the fifty tons of weed in the truck, Dread?"

"No worries, mon. I am a licensed Ganja Coordinator at the hotel. Management and the Babylon brass worked their thing, and I have free passage."

The cop peeked into the vehicle and waved the Rastaman through.

"I doubt they would arrest you, but if they found a gun on my skinny behind, it wouldn't be pretty. Like good night for me," Dread said.

"I got you," Illisya said.

"So, you're licensed to sell weed at the hotel?" Kali asked.

"Yeah. Management doesn't want guests wandering on the beach and dealing with unsavory characters."

"I heard you," Illisya said.

▲ ▲ ▲

Six months later, Kali stirred marinara sauce on the stove in her apartment when the phone rang. Detective Councell introduced himself as the officer leading the investigation into a string of strange rapes and murders and invited her to a police lineup.

Kali remembered him from when she reported the crime about eighteen months earlier. Another officer had overseen the case at the time.

"Hello, are you there, Ms. Falkner?" Councell asked.

"Oh yes, sir. What do you need me for, sir?"

"We apprehended a suspect who may be able to help us with your case."

"Oh."

"Will you come down to the precinct at two in the afternoon tomorrow?"

"Oh yes, I will, sir."

Kali hung up. Her knees wobbled, and she held onto the kitchen counter. She scrambled to Illisya's door, knocked, and entered.

"Guess what? The police want me to participate in a point-and-identify thingy."

"What type of lineup?" Illisya asked, closing her book.

"Jack O'Spade. Do you think he came back to life? They said extreme religious goons can..."

"You're required to take a shower before you go. Start now with a cold one," Illisya said.

"Illisya, what should I do?"

"No, it's not number one. No, it's not number two, or three, or four. At no point should you say, 'I know this because my friend and I butchered him in Negril, Jamaica,'" Illisya said.

"A wrong statement. You annihilated him, bitch. Do you think I'm dumb?"

"No, but you gloat. Keep it professional and somber."

"I'll wear my Iron Maiden face," Kali said.

"Oh, and may God help us."

Kali tackled her onto the bed, and they rolled in a tangle.

Kali kept her appointment at the station house the next day. She approached the Sergeant's desk anxiously.

"Can I help you, miss?" the officer asked.

"I have an appointment with Detective Councell."

"Wait over there. Someone will be with you."

Kali sat on a red plastic chair, fidgeting with her phone. Detective Hurtz, Councell's partner, opened the door to her right, holding a clipboard.

"Ms. Falkner, follow me this way."

Two distressed women passed her in the hall, sniffing and dabbing at their faces. Hurtz ushered her behind the one-way mirror.

Kali's eyes rifled over the four masked men in the lineup, and she turned away, head bowed.

"He's not there," Kali said.

Detective Councell opened the file in his hand and gawked at Kali.

"Okay, guys, let's hear it," Councell commanded.

"You can call me Jack O'Spade," number one said.

"No, not him," Kali said.

"Number two," Councell said.

"You can call me Jack O Spade."

"It's no use. I'm not able to help, officer, and those other two are the wrong body sizes."

She sniffed a couple of times.

"I want to go," Kali said.

She wanted to laugh out loud but knew Illisya would kill her.

Councell gazed at her back as she departed and noted that she had come with the preconceived notion that Jack O'Spade would not be in the lineup.

"So where is he, Ms. Kali Falkner? You know Jack's whereabouts. I saw it in your eyes and along the mocking lines around your mouth."

He wrote in his little book and caught a final glimpse of Kali as she disappeared through the door.

Chapter 8

Present Day

On a warm, star-filled Miami night, limousines and beautiful, expensive late-model cars pulled into a lighted mansion driveway in Bal Harbor. The Miami elite, dressed in their finest, bantered and streamed toward the mansion's front door.

Uniformed chauffeurs and valets gathered under a tree, chatting lightly. The moon hung like an exclusive molten glow, as if it enjoyed the laughter floating from the lit windows.

Headlights approached. A vehicle parked on the main road thirty yards away, and three doors slammed.

"The secondary cast members have arrived, folks," a chauffeur said.

"Oh, shut up, Manny," May said.

Illisya, the epitome of loveliness and class rode Bill's right arm as high-strung Kali snuggled on his left. The calm, beautiful night couldn't soothe Kali's troubled, war-zone-like aura. The three of them touched twenty-six, give or take, but Kali could pass for thirty-five.

Bill dwarfed the women in his expensive, ill-fitted suit, and the jovial trio strolled past the valets and chauffeurs up the torch-lit driveway.

Five minutes later, an expensive late-model sports car pulled up. Galvin removed a barricade and guided it into an exclusive reserved slot.

JW Dawes, the tycoon, hoisted his trimmed, polished, thirty-five-year-old body from the automobile. Life's nectar runneth over JW's cup a cognizant participant in the bounty, yet he remained grounded as a beautiful soul.

Galvin and May rushed to JW's car.

"Hi, JW, Mr. Dawes, lovely night, JW," the men and women said.

JW bumped fists and slapped friends' shoulders.

"We could be witnesses to the last perfect night here, people," JW said.

"I refuse to drop into a false sense of security, JW. It's gonna rain on someone's parade soon," Galvin said.

"Did what's-her-name ever return, Galvin?" JW asked.

"You're asking about Long Legs Susan, and she never did," Galvin said.

"He's still waiting for hers, and my legs are still too short," May said.

JW and May laughed at Galvin's expense.

"Well, I'll see you guys later," JW said.

JW strolled up the driveway, twirling his keys on his index finger.

"Mr. D., can I hold your keys? I wanna blow this baby out around the block for you," May said.

"Oh yeah, like you did the fellow in the back seat of my Bentley," JW said.

May bellowed, vulgar, and obscene.

"I called it an unfortunate accident a couple of ages ago," May said.

"Regina still shivers whenever she rode in the Bentley," JW said.

"Mars got flooded again today," May said.

JW tossed the keys, and May squealed as she caught them. She worked for JW until the backseat incident, and Regina fired her.

JW couldn't care less what she did and gave her a wink plus a fat check to march away into the morning sun.

A white-uniformed doorman manned the entrance, and from his appearance, he may never have experienced younger days.

No, my eyes are fooling me. The man must've been young at one point, JW supposed.

The aged man ushered JW into his host, Mrs. Lostrum's, warm embrace. Her exquisite evening gown transformed her into a youthful fifty-something. Mrs. Lostrum winked at JW; her eyes sparkled, and he kissed her hand.

"Don't you think money does beautiful things for a washed-up old hag, huh, JW?" Mrs. Lostrum asked.

"I always refute it when they say you put the B into the B-word," JW answered.

Mrs. Lostrum smooched him on the cheek.

"JW, darling, your company has always been delightful to my soul."

"The pleasure's all mine."

She escorted JW into a buzzing ballroom, where conversations clashed with laughter like two cymbals.

"Oh, I'm so sorry Regina is under the weather," Mrs. Lostrum said.

"It's a touch of the flu, and she sent her regards."

They waltzed into the massive ballroom, into the embrace of opulent, rapturous, overfed people and trimmings.

Fasper, a fat, middle-aged man, extended his hand to JW.

Mrs. Lostrum floated away, and Fasper shouted above the din.

"JW, old chap, I can still make good on the Zurich deal."

An impatient JW turned from Fasper and snagged a champagne flute from a server.

"Let's drink. Tomorrow breathes down our backs, already in possession of too many unknown layers," JW said.

JW pumped Lewis's arm with strength and sincere gusto. Lewis wore Maddy, a beautiful young woman, on his other arm.

"How're you doing, Lewis?" JW asked.

Lewis peeked at Maddy as if to say, *Are you blind, old chap?*

"How could I possibly do any better?" Lewis answered.

JW shook Maddy's dainty hand.

"Not here on Earth, old friend," JW said.

Maddy smiled and sprayed enough sugar to sweeten the world.

"Thank you, JW," Maddy said.

JW surveyed the room and waved to Bill with Illisya, the strange, enigmatic beauty on his arm.

"Damn, where did Bill find an angel who disguised her wings and heavenly accessories? Doesn't she know those of us with eyes can still see?"

JW caught an associate's attention and drifted away into the crowd.

▲ ▲ ▲

A shadow shuffled behind a shrub, and a Sad-Face Bum hobbled along the hedgerow and peeked into the dimness beneath the trees fifteen yards from the mansion. Galvin strolled down a concrete walkway by variegated rose bushes under multicolored lights. The octogenarian in bright red rags peeked through a window.

"Hey," Galvin said.

The Sad-Face Bum shuffled across the lawn, and Galvin stood frozen in a profound, introspective moment.

His parents taught him never to disrespect the least of humanity, especially those you are notches above on the physical plane. You are never far from humankind, regardless of how long you reside on or travel Infinity's high road.

"Damn, I should've offered the man a few dollars. He may be hungry."

Galvin's eyes scoured the ground, but the Sad-Face Bum had disappeared. He wondered how the man generated the speed to cross the broad lawn and vanish. Galvin ran in the direction the man went, but the man in rags was gone.

▲ ▲ ▲

The cocktail party broke into heated discussion groups across the ballroom floor. Illisya's classy beauty lingered in JW's mind and cut deep into his being. His attention held her without pretense at every opening. At one point, Illisya smiled and lit the world as evolution intended it to shine thousands of years ago.

"She's an employee's woman and must only be admired from a distance," JW told himself.

He reached for a champagne flute and glanced at Illisya as he raised it to his lips.

Kali sunk her eyes into Blake, a born linebacker type who mingled across the room and winked at Illisya.

"I'm the quarterback, and I feel the need to be tackled," Kali said.

"You go right ahead and get bruised," Illisya said.

Illisya smirked as Kali stalked across the room toward Blake like a cat closing in on prey.

Illisya intercepted a server, and lustful, envious eyes followed her across the floor.

She chuckled under her breath.

"If I didn't have JW to snare, I could walk the red carpet in Hollywood every weekday and twice on Sundays."

She drank in the adoration to the minutest detail, devoid of pretense, and lifted the champagne flute to her lips but barely tasted the bubbles.

Bill reached for Illisya, and she waltzed into his arms.

"Billy Boy, you hit the nail and not your fingers. Your boss is present and better yet, no wife. Life's so sweet when prodded."

"Should I gloat?" Bill asked.

"No. Do what I paid you for and introduce me to your boss. And please don't be too obvious."

"Why am I doing this again?"

"Billy, endless dreaming only points you in the general direction of Heaven."

Her words deflated him.

"Please, darling, don't take it too hard. You'll be rich one day, but I'll be too damn old, of course."

Illisya smiled, warming Bill's inner being for a fleeting second.

"You'll be chasing whores born this very hour, Billy Boy."

Bill maneuvered her toward JW, his brow still heavy, but his mind lighter.

"Don't go brand new on me, Billy Boy."

"One of your old gym shorts shot my ego years ago."

Illisya slipped an arm around Bill's waist, and his grin expanded to the size of a planet's birth. A server passed, Bill handed Illisya a fresh drink, smitten to a pulp, though he knew she only pretended to drink.

Illisya's vibrant spirit bubbled. She surveyed the room, caught JW's eye, and flashed him a sweet, brief smile.

Kali winked at Illisya and departed on Blake's arm. Illisya waited until they disappeared through the door and sighed. She hoped Kali would retire early, and she did.

"Okay, Billy Boy, it's showtime."

Bill guided Illisya toward JW.

A Distinguished Gent lurked in the corner and eyed Bill as he made the introduction. The Gent's eerie dark eyes twinkled, and his fifty-five-year-old facial lines deepened, lending an unnatural intensity to his gaze.

"JW, say hello to the lovely Illisya Haynes," Bill said.

Bill's broad shoulders blotted out the man's stare.

JW petted Illisya's arm and smiled into her eyes with the confidence of a supreme alpha. Her smirk lingered like an inviting light on his face. Her beauty and elegance held him like an elemental magnet.

"JW, you're a master of situations. I'm leaving you in the line of fire," Bill said.

Bill winked above Illisya's head and disappeared into the crowd.

"It's a pleasure meeting a man of your stature off-screen and in the flesh," Illisya said.

"I guess that's how you soften steel?" JW asked.

"Oh no, on the contrary. Hard is primal."

"Something tells me you do spells."

"I've been known to dabble," Illisya quipped.

Mrs. Lostrum swept in and seized JW's arm.

"Sorry, Sugar, there's someone JW must meet."

"Miss Haynes, I insist I run into you again later," JW said.

Illisya winked as JW departed.

"Folks, I heard the wonderful sound of thunder. Or is it the bubbly stuff in the flute eating at my brain cells?" Illisya mumbled.

Illisya practiced an alcohol, and drug-free lifestyle, except for a social sip. She considered herself a huntress with sharp edges, that never dulled.

Two former cocktail party queens eyed her from across the room.

"I sold my soul to the Devil, and I cannot compare to yonder bitch," said the Tom Ford.

"Hush, we've got the money. She's indigent," said the McQueen V-neck.

"That's the ugly in the room. Money should've bought us more. Pray tell, how do you know she's indigent?"

"I can tell from the glow emanating from her. If she owned a bag, the burden of keeping it or accumulating more, would steal some of her radiance."

"You mean the glint bright as the sun and loud as a siren calling men?"

A smart young basketball player crossed their sightline.

"Do you ever shoot hoops with new money?" the Tom Ford asked.

"I heard they run up and down the court."

"Let's go flagrant-foul his ass."

They moved toward one of the Miami Heat's young superstars as the games of life danced across the stage in vivid disguise on a hot South Florida night.

Chapter 9

Blake and Kali stumbled to his car in a tight embrace a block from the mansion. He pecked her lips like an assessment exercise, kissed her, and wrapped his massive arms around her as if he wanted to absorb her body. His hand dropped below her belly button, and Kali giggled.

Minutes later, Blake's car sped away, and a black sedan lurking in the pall followed at a professional distance. Homicide Detective Sergeant Dave Councell hunched over the wheel.

Councell carried an intensity in his eyes as if he had not blinked all day, and it furrowed his forty-three-year-old brow. One would think he had run his face through the machine used to manufacture the world's unpleasantness.

His partner, Detective Karolina Hurtz, wore a cheery expression and buttoned her lips against the intensity in Councell's stare. A mocking, joyous feeling transformed her forty-year-old face into a sweet thirty-something gem.

A zealous Office Council hunted Kali after the police lineup. Hurtz begged him to close the case based on his conviction. He believed Kali Falkner murdered Jack O'Spade or knew who did it. Hurtz eyed the lighted buildings from the shotgun seat like a child playing road trip games.

Councell glued his eyes to Blake's taillights, and his excitement rose.

Is it happening at last? Did she strike tonight? Did the trauma of the assault trigger inner demons and warp the poor rich girl into a murderer?

Councell's heart pounded like a rock against his chest.

"The murdering bitch will strike tonight, and I shall catch her red handed and close this case."

"Do we not need an exclusive permit to question anyone living in these neighborhoods?" Hurtz asked.

"Do not allow what is inside your head to shackle you, Hurtz."

"What exactly do you have against little broken front rich girls, Councell?"

"I will tell you again. She murdered Jack O'Spade and took us for fools."

"Do you have evidence to back up your story?"

"Jack O'Spade is dead. How else could she so effortlessly slight the men in the lineup? Do you know why? She organized his demise."

Hurtz glanced at his stern profile.

"The flippant tone of her voice on the phone when I invited her said volumes to me. She fought not to laugh in our faces," Councell said.

"Jack O'Spade was a rapist and a murderer," Hurtz said.

"Why do we have laws? Do not all those victims need closure?" Councell asked.

Hurtz held her tongue and shifted her back to find a sweet spot in the seat.

"Her murderous butt is mine," Councell continued.

Blake's car pulled into a driveway in a multimillionaire neighborhood, a short ride from the billion-dollar enclave where he attended the party.

"Someone beat you to her, it seems," Hurtz joked.

Councell parked farther down on a Lane, and a bored Hurtz yawned.

The department had no idea how many women Jack O'Spade abused and would never know the exact figure. His victims suffered in silence and anonymity instead of coming forward. Hurtz took on the sordid affair personally. If the Falkner girl ridded the world of an evil individual, I say kudos to her.

"I sense what you are thinking, but it may not have been self-defense. I suspect she did it in cold blood," Councell said.

"What methods of detection led you to that conclusion?" Hurtz asked.

"There is no history of him raping the same woman twice."

"Benghazi reminds me of what men do on dry nights," Hurtz snapped.

Councell wanted to give her an evil eye but could not afford to peel his gaze away from the lighted window of the mansion. Hurtz yawned again and fidgeted into a new position.

"You are my partner. I will indulge you and your dead milk hunch."

Hurtz grew up in Buffalo, New York, until her early teens, when her mother divorced her detective father. She never knew whether art imitated life or life aped mass media. Statistics claim that every law enforcement officer on television or in films juggles home problems alongside the job, most ending in separation.

Come to think of it, what husband of mine would lie in bed night after night while I patrolled dark places with another man? He would never think of the bullets and knives I dodged to bring home my gold pot intact.

After the divorce, her father moved to New York City and joined the NYPD. Hurtz loved and admired him and sympathized with her mother's pain. Despite the turmoil, she wanted to join the department from the age of eleven and decided that permanent residency with her mother might dampen her dreams. She traveled by bus every other weekend to visit her father. He indulged her in law enforcement techniques, broke protocol, and sometimes took her to crime scenes. They kept it secret from her mother as he taught her everything about the job and reinforced her resolve.

Fresh out of the academy, Hurtz hurdled the relationship pains that dogged dedicated officers and remained single. Two or three times per month, she went on what she called service jobs, initiated the liaison, and said goodbye in stone at dawn. Moving to South Florida, where she could conduct a stakeout without freezing, ranked among her most significant achievements.

Hurtz and her partner shared a respectful and knowledgeable alliance. She recalled the embarrassing Williamson case, where she swore the woman murdered her husband. Councell exhibited patience, waited her out, and nudged her toward the suspect, a one-hit singer. Guilt devoured the man, and during his first interview, he confessed.

Hurtz glanced at her partner's stern profile. They never gloated over each other's mistakes. The suspect sang his admission from the lowest bass to the highest falsetto notes on the ride to jail, and Councell never once gave her a knowing look.

Hurtz adjusted her weapon and folded her arms.

Thank you for Miami's warm weather, Mr. Big Man.

Chapter 10

In the ensuing weeks, JW, Regina, a gorgeous and elegant woman of thirty-four, and six-year-old Mary chased and captured a beautiful, hurricane-free summer for themselves. The regular South Florida midday shower pelted Fletcher Island, and Mary ran onto the mansion patio in a bathing suit and sneakers.

"Mary waited. I want to check the sky for lightning," Regina called.

Mary picked up a soccer ball from the rack.

"Mom, the sky is electricity free, and the sun played with the rain like it did yesterday."

"I am coming, dear."

Regina stepped out in faded sweats. She marveled at the interplay of sun and rain and raced onto the lawn.

"Not fair," Mary cried.

Mary kicked the ball high toward the mini goal, and JW raced from around the house, dribbled, and nailed a shot. The ball swerved, crashed into the wall, rebounded, and Regina headed it into the net.

"One for the mummy, girl."

Mary dummied JW, and he fell on his butt in the wet grass as she scored.

"One for the baby child."

"It is on, it is on, I tell you," JW bellowed.

Regina dribbled toward the goal, chased by Mary and JW, as the sun gave way and the shower thickened.

Mary frolicked on the beach one afternoon while her parents kept watchful eyes and sipped tall, ice-cold drinks in the shade. JW, the tycoon, and his family spent quality time together daily. Investors may have been unaware that he had left their money in the multiverse, where each dollar multiplied itself, much like living cells.

Illisya wore a forty-year-old woman disguise, capped with a giant straw hat, and sat four tables away from JW, Regina, and Mary at the South Beach Café. She ordered and sipped a muddy, fruity drink beneath the wide brim. For the past four days, JW and his family have been playing on the grounds of their mansion on Fisher Island, and she could not get close enough to spy on them, so she did so from a skiff on the water.

After the late lunch, Illisya tailed the Dawes to Terminal Island Road and fished out her spyglasses as they boarded the Fisher Island ferry.

Mary danced on the ferry deck, and her parents left the comfort of their vehicle and indulged her wild steps. Illisya tagged Regina as she and Mary pointed at unusual crimson cloud formations in the western sky.

JW and Regina attended every official social event on the seasonal chart and never missed an opportunity to dance.

On an enhanced South Florida night, a midnight platinum moon bathed the Dawes mansion and grounds in a fantastic silver glow. JW's Bentley braked in the driveway as the gates closed.

Regina bolted from the car barefoot across the lawn and shed her flowing gown as she ran. Regina's mother, an avid reader of erotic books, hid her treasures from the children. Regina raided her stashes and read them from the age of fourteen. In adulthood, she replayed scenes from those pages to spice her marriage.

JW trailed her around the flower bed as she tossed her panties onto a rose bush. He stripped to his underwear and lunged at her. Regina evaded him, giggled, and raced back to the car.

She braced her hands against the door, arched her back, and widened her legs.

▲ ▲ ▲

JW and his family brunched at Café Nikki on Ocean Drive, where the water mimicked light turquoise on a flawless sunny day. After the meal, he dropped Regina and Mary at the ferry depot and drove to the Government Center parking lot on Northwest First Street. He hailed a taxi.

The cab traveled south for half an hour and dropped JW on a tree-lined Southwest Twenty Third Avenue. Wearing a hooded sweatshirt, he walked two blocks along the quiet avenue, keyed into a gated community, and knocked on an apartment door. A blonde in lingerie answered and posed inside the threshold. She gave JW's eyes time to feast on her beauty before running into his arms.

Five days later, inside a white picket fence house in Miami Gardens, a dreadlocked woman undressed for JW to heavy bass and drum music. Six pairs of multicolored iron scrubs hung on a rack, with the word Doctor printed on a tag on the first in line. JW stood legs apart, blocking the name. His hands sank into his pockets, his eyes blazed, and he rocked his waistline as the woman danced.

▲ ▲ ▲

At nine fifteen the next morning, JW and his upper-floor employees chatted about headlines, joked, and laughed in a communal area for ten minutes. After a hot cup of coffee and a croissant, JW retreated to his office.

At nine forty-five, Illisya's clunker pulled into JW's parking lot, and her fabulous red dress stunned onlookers as she exited the vehicle. Her gait and expression said she was the one who drove the Bentley parked beside the Gremlin.

She paused to admire JW's monument of success, gave it a sweet look, inhaled, exhaled, and strode toward the entrance with purpose.

The Sad Bum shuffled across her path from behind a minibus, and she missed a step to avoid colliding with him.

"Good day to you, sir. How are you today?"

The Sad Bum shuffled on, obliviously. Illisya stared after him, drawn as though the man in red rags traveled beside her on a dangerous journey.

▲ ▲ ▲

Illisya tapped her right foot in the elevator to an internal rhythm. She stepped out onto the twentieth floor and approached Dotti Brown, a cute red-haired Black woman her age.

The secretary's beauty sparked a running thought in Illisya's mind. She would enjoy exploring the extracurricular activities JW and his staff conducted after hours. It was a given that when she became Mrs. Dawes, employees like Dotti Too Cute Reds would need new employment.

"Illisya Haynes, ma'am. I have an appointment."

"Good morning, JW. Miss Haynes is here, sir, a bit early," Brown said into her mouthpiece.

She beamed at Illisya. Damn, those are fine chewers in her mouth, Illisya noted. Whiter than snow. She will be casualty number one when I take over.

Dotti came around her workstation and ushered Illisya into JW's private office.

I envisioned the eye magnet ass before she stood.

Illisya counted her chickens before the hatched eggs behind Dotti Brown.

JW rose and extended his hand. Illisya shook it like a fish snapping at juicy bait.

"Please be seated, Miss Haynes."

"You can call me Illisya, JW."

"I am curious about your business proposition," JW said.

Illisya's eyes rifled the office as JW watched her appraisal. Satisfied, she perched on his polished hardwood desk.

"Well, I am a twenty-six-year-old virgin."

Her eyes needled him.

"From birth, I have eaten oxygen as a female."

She crossed and uncrossed her legs. JW leaned back in his leather armchair, amused beyond fascination.

"I have no plans to compete with existing foundations," Illisya said.

"Why have I been told all your cherished secrets?" JW asked.

Illisya threw her head back and laughed.

"Well, mine fell far from immaculate. Regardless of the blight, I claim planet Earth as my reward."

"Illisya, if you seek employment?"

"Sometimes we are grounded when we should be airborne, but settle for less, never."

"How can I help you?"

"I am afraid you misunderstood me."

"Did I?"

"Yes. I aim for a penthouse, an expensive sports car, and at least twenty thousand dollars of bitch money per month in my near future."

JW leaned forward, his eyes urging her onward.

"I have never experienced a neon light proposition or seduction. I have no intention of doing a day's work unless it is bedroom related."

"The question I need to ask about the eviction. Do you want to make a stop before the mental institution, or will a kick to the curb by my people suffice?" JW asked.

"I vowed myself to one man."

The intercom chimed.

"Excuse me, Mr. Dawes. I placed your ten fifteen in room five, sir."

"I think I should powder my nose," Illisya said.

"Follow me."

▲ ▲ ▲

Van Drake, JW's hawk-eyed Security Chief, perched on the edge of the table in room five and waited for JW. Hard years in jail could not have carved rougher lines into his face. JW entered, and Drake's fifty-two-year-old butt wiggled for a sweet spot.

"What do you have?" JW asked.

Van flipped his folder.

"She's clean. No close friends except for Bill and Kali Falkner. She graduated head of her class and spent considerable time in the company of an old woman named Meg Foster."

"They seldom can reproduce those forms in bed. How far back did you dig?"

"We went back to her middle school days."

JW reached for the file and flicked through the pages.

"Who do you think Meg Foster is to her? Not a blood relative?" JW asked.

"Her mother's best friend, and they taught together for years."

JW inspected Meg's photo.

"A beautiful woman in her younger years, but bitterness and protracted time left nasty marks around her mouth," JW said.

"My thoughts exactly."

"I'll catch you later, man," JW said.

"Aren't you the lucky one," Van chuckled.

Six years ago, Drake shot and injured a fellow officer while the man choked a talented high school athlete to death in a back alley. The news networks called it an extraordinary, unduplicated act on this side of the second coming. A week after the incident, JW offered Drake a job. The young man grew into a star quarterback for one of the top NFL teams in the league. Van Drake never missed one of his games when he played in town, and the boy insisted he should not.

▲ ▲ ▲

Illisya sat on JW's desk. JW fished two bottles of water from his refrigerator.

"Do you want some water?" JW asked.

"No, thanks."

"Sorry about the interruption. The road is long, and one can only see so far down it," JW said.

"I came seconds away from saying, JW Dawes, you're the only man for me before the interruption."

He held the water bottle two inches from his mouth and gawked at her. She rose, posed, and buried her eyes into JW like a fork into a juicy steak.

"I'm a happily married man. What made you believe I'd have any part in your proposal?" JW asked.

Illisya plopped back before him.

"Wealthy, strong, influential men existed to conquer and turned us girls into loyal whores, lest we wasted away in the beds of lesser males or females," Illisya said.

JW grinned.

"Time and circumstances have suppressed the fire in weak men. However, males are beasts of prey, created to dominate and devour as they saw fit," Illisya continued.

Illisya bent over inches from JW.

"I don't want to shout it, but I'm one of the fireless ones," JW said.

"I would have seen the paunch, dull eyes, and ugly shoes."

JW chuckled and stole a glimpse at his feet.

"I doubt therapy would help you," JW said.

"Throughout history, one woman never satisfied alpha studs like yourself. I mean fellows who mastered the King David Syndrome."

JW's eyes widened.

"Did you say King David Syndrome?" JW asked.

"Are you familiar with the term?"

"Are rooftops a piece of the promise?" JW inquired.

He glanced away, and his eyes snapped back into Illisya's bosom. She jumped to her feet and pivoted.

"On the home front, I flew invisibly. Nevertheless, I traveled well if you're flying overseas or out of town," Illisya boasted.

An amused JW relaxed back, hooked, hot, and ready to burn the door.

"I bet you do. Nonetheless, I'm beyond empty heads."

Illisya slapped her midriff.

"I can quote from either *Sound Bites* or *The Destroyers of Time*. What's your preference? I have two master's degrees somewhere under my belt. You can dig for them. My IQ also stood two points below yours for the sake of this conversation."

"What does the word profiling mean to you?" JW asked.

"It's a pitiful law enforcement term already," Illisya said.

Illisya's face lit like a furnace from JW's point of view. She posed a hand at her side, and her dress fell in a bundle on the floor.

"My degrees are due for fine tuning, and don't be gentle about it either. I'm a virgin, not an infant," Illisya quipped.

She leaned her upper body over the desk, and he buried his attention in her bosom.

"Miss Brown, my meeting has extended further than I anticipated. Please hold my calls."

"Yes, sir."

Illisya turned her back to JW and rested her backside six inches from the desk's edge. JW hurried to her, and she wrapped her legs around his waist and met his lips.

"Don't hold back now. I'm a virgin, not a baby," Illisya said.

She breathed heat like a dragon, fell onto her back, and JW grasped her airborne ankles.

Chapter 11

The meteorologists across a dozen platforms forecast 60 degrees for Miami on a dreary, cloudy day. The natives broke out their sweaters, light leather jackets, and boots against the chilly northern invader.

Illisya's BMW 850i Coupe and the Distinguished Gent's Bentley pulled into a service station seconds apart.

Two months evaporated behind her like vehicle exhaust into her conquer-and-devour mission in what mere Golddiggers would mislabel as milking a billionaire.

She scanned the man, riffled the auto with her eyes, and dropped her gaze back to the gas nozzle in her hand.

The Distinguished Gent aimed his sight above Illisya's head and smirked. His eyes hid his intentions but held diabolical mysteries like harbingers. She ignored him, for distraction didn't factor into the world she built and dreamed of, paved with diamonds and gold. The scent of the two new cars assaulted her nostrils, and she inhaled a ton of it from a gust of wind as it passed through the Bentley's open doors and windows.

They should bottle the seducing fragrance and place it on the market as a scent of success. Illisya's soon-to-be status as a billionaire dissuaded her from such a venture.

As the Bentley pulled away, she caught the driver in her peripheral vision, and her heart kicked against her breast. Her stylish denim jacket and loose-fit sweater generated unnatural heat in the chilly wind for a moment. Illisya retrieved her card from the pump, sat in her warm seat, and inhaled the new leather aroma in the morning of her future.

▲ ▲ ▲

Mrs. Gibson pulled into her driveway, and Ron Gibson alighted, stretched his arm muscles over his head, and glanced over at Meg's house. In moments of clarity during the last two weeks at the VA hospital in his PTSD treatment sessions, he wondered who helped his old friend with her lawn. The Marine Corps discharged him six years ago, and he nursed severe mental issues at twenty-eight. He stood like a statue at his bedroom window, and a gust of wind stirred trash on Meg's driveway like a whirlwind.

The fire-red Bentley drove by. The leaves changed direction and rotated counterclockwise. The phenomenon marveled Ron. Last month, he ran out of meds for days, and a Miccosukee Indian war party rode by nude on M1A1 tanks. The next day, he ran into an aircraft carrier on the pond in the park after heavy rains, but a Bentley on his block, never.

"Last week I sneaked through Heaven and ran through Hell, but never a Bentley on my block."

Illisya's BMW roared through Meg's broken gate amid airborne leaves, and she bounced from the automobile on her toes. She removed grocery bags from the trunk, paused, and swiveled her head toward Ron's window. Ron ducked in time and crawled away on his knees into the recess of the dark room.

Meg opened the front door, gaped down at Illisya, and placed a surprised hand over her mouth.

"Meg Foster girl, how's it?"

Meg's face broke into a grin.

"I'm old, dying, and lack sexual feelings. Why don't you come the hell inside and bring whatever the fuck you brought along? Enough of the fucking stupid questions."

"Wow, and I forgot to pick up some hemorrhoid medicine," Illisya said.

"Go to hell, hoe."

Meg held the rickety screen door, and Illisya squeezed by her into a neat, clean-living space. Lavender's scent stung her nostrils, and they made quick adjustments.

Black candles burned in ebony candelabras everywhere, and ebony curtains were drawn like tight drum strings. Meg turned the four jet-colored chairs back to the black-clothed dining table years ago, and they remained in place. Midnight chinaware was set for two, dusted, and all the seats in Meg's home faced or rested against the walls incorrectly. Illisya led Meg into the all-ebony, sterilized kitchen, and she unpacked groceries.

Illisya painted the newest coat of raven-colored paint last year and reveled in the doomsday shade herself. She brought into Meg's narrative that the melanic color rejuvenated depleted souls. Old Meg placed her elbows on the counter and monitored Illisya at work.

"You're the daughter I never birthed," Meg said.

"I'm honored, but I thought I meant more to you. Why sweat it? Chill, girl."

"I'll not have thee address me in clichés," Meg said.

"I thought platitudes enjoyed their day back in your time, in the fourteen centuries?"

"Your runaway cheapskate mother should have gotten you up to speed."

"By the time I hit ten, I covered her debt to you," Illisya said.

"Bring my George back to life, and I'll think about it."

"You have got the Viet Cong, and I mixed up in colors," Illisya quipped.

Illisya wiped the counter and grinned at Meg.

"You should've remarried, old girl."

"I couldn't have other men touch me after my George. We got married on a beautiful morning. He spent two nights with me, flew out, and died a week later," Meg groaned.

Illisya turned to her.

"You never did it again?"

"Never. I blamed the world for the havoc, death, and destruction of souls and beliefs. Long after I'm gone, the fuck storm rages on all platforms."

Illisya smiled and handed Meg a small bag.

"I followed. You want to deny us the right to scheme, love, murder, and elect idiots to represent us?" Illisya said.

"Damn, it's not only my old ass that's in constant pain."

"Yeah, we're busy on all roads."

"Lord, give me the strength to slap this girl's front into some young man's parlor."

"They left you in the viral back bush. The authorities have downgraded battered gals. Please enjoy your new miracle arthritis drugs."

"I hope the side effects don't make me piss from my ears. Now, find yourself a suitable man," Meg said.

"I'm riding the long road home as we speak."

"You're a cagey little closet hoe. You weren't gonna say crap to me."

"Trip not, it's a four-point plan, and I considered phase one a mighty success," Illisya quipped.

"What the hell do you mean?"

"I bet you haven't eaten anything of substance all day," Illisya said.

"Huh? Are you changing the subject?"

"Yeah, I think I should fix you a meal right now."

"Great move, but I hope you can multi-task, cook, and spill the juicy shit."

"Well, I've mislaid my virginity, and I'm going to marry the guy who ripped it to shreds."

Meg's face lit up.

"It's about time you utilized your ass. What about the new ride?"

"Someone is still scrolling down to the fine print."

Illisya caught the water in a pot, winked, and chuckled at Meg's bulbed eyes.

▲ ▲ ▲

Ron paced in his room with a broom and a dustpan. He lingered at the window and gazed at Illisya's car, and tears ran down his cheeks like mountain streams. Ron guffawed, backed away, and flicked on the lights. He laughed, and his muscles tightened when he emitted unholy sounds on the march around the spacious space.

Behind him, a photo frame turned backward against the mirror on the dusty dresser, and vials of pills stood and lay on their sides in disarray around it.

Mrs. Gibson pushed a head of gray hair through the door.

"Ron, what the hell's going on in here?"

"Nothing, Mom, we're patrolling up and down and back and forth across the world."

"Sweet hon, journey quietly, and remember to take your medication on time."

"Yes, I will, but a day in the city is a day in the universe."

Mrs. Gibson closed the door. Ron beamed like a child on Christmas morning and rubbed his eager palms together.

He retrieved paints and brushes from a closet and painted an angel, a demon, and a devil in vivid colors, arm in arm, on the right wall. His strokes swiped like a windshield wiper on extra-high settings. On the ceiling, he painted saints in suits, honed swords, and oiled guns. Behind him, a dozen multicolored pills, two syringes, three beers, five soda cans, and a baby smoking a joint in a puddle of blood decorated the partition.

Ron picked up the photo frame, blew on it, cleaned it with his shirttail, and removed the dust from his and Lacey's faces locked in an embrace in their Marine regalia. The camera caught their wedding bands on their fingers.

He swallowed four pills and turned to a lifelike Humvee on fire on the back wall, hurried up a ladder. Ron sketched the Sad Bum in a golden light and the Distinguished Gent in his red Bentley below the Humvee and sang.

"One day in the city is a day in the universe. We're miles apart, sharing the same experiences. Oh, life is a chain of thought."

Chapter 12

At 3:01, bubbly Mary Dawes and her friends waited in the pickup pen at her private school on SW 1st Avenue in Brickell, a quiet residential avenue. Their parents' autos lined up in the pickup lane, and teachers ushered the five- to seven-year-old children into the vehicles. Mary bounced on her toes, and her eyes searched for her Mom's SUV.

A dark-windowed, raggedy, rusty brown early-model Coupe parked two blocks up, and the unseen driver monitored the operation. Rust blanketed the original paint job, and putty held the panels together.

Mrs. Regina Dawes' SUV pulled up in line, picked up her daughter, and the watcher tailed her.

▲ ▲ ▲

JW stood at his office window and gazed across the bay at the South Beach buildings of success. To his left, the downtown high-rises glistened in brilliant sunlight. The expression on his face mellowed, and a decisive sheen appeared around his eyes. One could call it love, war, or something in between.

His phone rang behind him on his desk; he stepped back and punched the speaker, annoyed at the uninvited intrusion that broke his thoughts.

"JW, it's me," a timid voice said.

He sat in his deep, comfortable chair, and his body relaxed.

"Could you please get on with it, Dimitri?"

"He's making his move on Wymax on Thursday."

"That's tomorrow, Dimitri."

"They kept it under heavy metal."

"Another C rolls down the hill and his third hostile takeover in two years," JW said.

"Dump all your stocks now and remember who delivered the info. I've got to run."

"I've got a good memory, son," JW said.

"Ms. Brown informed all the portfolio heads to sell everything we have on Wymax International and bought DBSX Global shares."

"Will do, sir."

"Set a meeting for all HD at three pm tomorrow and update your personal portfolio."

"Thank you, Mr. Dawes."

JW hung up, pondered, took a burnt phone from a secret compartment in his desk, and dialed.

"Hello, JW."

"Carol, it's time. I won't see you anymore."

Carol's voice cracked and exuded shock and desperation.

"Oh my God, JW, it's so unexpected. What am I gonna do? Where am I gonna live?"

"Carol, if someone lived in an apartment for over two years without paying rent or a lease, wouldn't you say she owned the place?"

"What do you mean?"

"Yes, the papers are in the mail, and a fat bonus sleeps in your account. Marry a fine man, Carol, and have beautiful babies. I'll always be your friend. Have a wonderful life."

JW cut the call and re-dialed.

"Tiffany—"

He wetted his lips in anticipation as his mind transferred Carol and Tiffany's time to Illisya.

▲ ▲ ▲

Mrs. Dawes pulled into the reserved parking space beside her husband's car. The watcher's car cruised by and disappeared up the road.

Mary Dawes sprinted into JW's office minutes later, ahead of Mrs. Dawes.

"Daddeee."

Mary ran into JW's arms. Mrs. Dawes untangled Mary, kissed JW on the lips, perched on the desk in Illisya's spot, and crossed her legs.

"How did they treat you in school today, honey?" JW asked.

"Excellent, Daddy, and we made a stop in every country of the world online this morning."

"Wow, honey, that's so cool," JW said.

"I think she's ready for her high-powered tablet," Regina said.

Mary's innocent eyes dug into her father's face, and she nodded five times.

"Let's go, let's go, Daddy. I'm done with the kid machine."

"Okay, let's go, big lady."

Mary planted a sloppy kiss on JW's jaw, leaped from his lap, and launched into her rhythmic, happy dance routine.

"I'm so happy. I love you, Daddy. You're the best."

Mary pulled JW's hand toward the door.

"Did you butter her tongue, Regina?"

"Hon, you've got to get up to speed. Lips come buttered these days."

"You don't say," JW said.

▲ ▲ ▲

They say there are days in Southern Florida when fish sweat from the heat, and the gators order ice by the ton. The day after the Stalker trailed Mary and her Mom was one such day. Detective Councell cranked his AC gauge to the max in a café's parking lot on Collings Avenue. Councell turned his eyes to the entrance of the café, and a bored Hurtz fiddled with her phone.

"What's the definition of obsession, Councell?"

"Is that what they call dedication to duty these days?"

Hurtz gaped at him above her glasses.

"The women of this city deserve peace of mind and fearless nights. Don't you think?" Councell asked.

"Jack O'Spade has not been heard from in over a year."

"Lack of information does not help the terrified to sleep. If anything, it gives his victims the jitters," Councell said.

Hurtz peeked into her binoculars, tagged Illisya and Kali at a window table, and favored Illisya for a long minute.

"If you hunted the other piece of work with the Falkner girl, I would understand."

He took the glasses from Hurtz.

"I want to recover Jack O'Spade's body. I want closure for all his victims. And what's wrong if Miss Beautiful there rides a rich friend's coattail?" Councell asked.

"She shivered in the sun, or daylight shivered at the sight of her. Don't you see the razors and bear traps at the edges of her eyes and mouth?"

Councell gaped across at Hurtz.

"Are you jealous, Hurtz?"

"You've reinforced what I always believed. You don't know much about women. But that's a whole different life for you."

"What about the one at home?" Councell asked.

"Which one, which home? She'd be your wife, and there is a difference between flying and caged birds."

"I heard you ran into admission issues at the convent gate."

"Motherfuckers checked for virginity," Hurtz snapped.

He drove off and muffled a smile.

Will I ever win an argument with a woman at home or work? I loved Hurtz like a mother or a sister. She possessed a sixth sense beyond my perception. Nevertheless, I marked her as off base in this case. Kali Falkner murdered Jack O'Spade, and I need the whereabouts of the body from her.

Kali wiped her mouth, dug in her pocketbook, and applied fresh lipstick.

"You sat there with a smug on your face. I'm going to pick up Dread at the airport," Kali said.

"How long will he be staying for?"

"I hope a thousand years. I'm gonna settle down with him."

"Damn, are you sure?"

"Who the hell knows about these things? People hook up, and time either strengthens or weakens the fuck thing they got going," Kali said.

"I couldn't have said it better, dear."

Kali got up and waved to the server.

"Plug front, bitch."

Illisya smiled up at her.

▲ ▲ ▲

JW's merry employees stood before stock market monitors on Thursday afternoon and cheered as DBSX Global stocks skyrocketed. The takeover hit the airwaves mid-morning, and the stock rose from twenty-two dollars to one hundred nineteen. A hubbub of voices filled the space, and people outshouted each other.

The party atmosphere in the boardroom needed only strippers. JW knocked his flute with his pen and got everyone's attention.

"Drink your wet stuff and drift back to work mode. We fire-sale at one hundred thirty dollars."

The champagne flutes climbed high, and the liquid dunked.

"Yes," the house shouted in unison.

Chapter 13

Sunlight blanketed the western side of Illisya's penthouse down to the ground floor over a serene Biscayne Bay. Residents sipped tall drinks and exchanged banter in lounge chairs on the eastern side under umbrellas.

Illisya painted the interior of her penthouse in cool cream colors and hung pinned silk murals of the great cats in various attack modes on her four living room walls. She struggled through the door, burdened by heavy department-store shopping bags, set them on the coffee table, ogled the cats like distant relatives' photographs, giggled, and headed down the hall.

In the late evening, rays fought the western blinds and couldn't find a peephole to inspect the carry-on inside the apartment. However, the penthouse's soft lighting enhanced its spacious, contemporary furniture. In the heavens, a spiteful dark cloud masked the sun's dying rays on their way home for the day.

Inside the bedroom, the king-size bedspread depicted a panoramic scene of lions feeding on a gazelle, complete with all the gory details and ugliness from the original drone photo shoot.

Someone splashed water in the bathroom, and Illisya sang from the Jacuzzi in a sweet, husky, bluesy voice.

"I ran with bloody and brutal lions on the hunt, but never for fun. We fed and slipped away, for in an instant, hunters can become prey."

She tilted her head back, her expression serene and angel-like in the warm water.

"I ran with bloody—"

Her phone lit up on the nightstand, and she pressed the speaker.

"Hello, hon."

"Are you sure it's me?" JW asked on the speakerphone.

"Darling, no one else has this number."

"I'm rushing in hot before you give it to someone else."

"It will never happen, baby, but make haste."

An inaudible mutter came from JW's end. Illisya giggled, and her hand dropped into the water.

"I'm doing it right now."

"I've known a dozen women apart from Regina. But you struck me like bricks by the ton."

"I'm one of the new designers' high-tech women. We stick to omega men like dirt in coal mines."

"You employed the steel softener as lead again," JW said.

"I beseech you to come in hard."

JW laughed, and it reverberated.

Illisya rushed out of the water in the nude and carefully removed each of the cats' murals, hid them in a closet, and hung Devin Abrams' and Paul Andrus' abstracts.

JW pulled beside Illisya's car in a company SUV and sat with his live phone on the console. The song "One Day in the City" pumped from the high-end stereo system. He leaned his head back and absorbed the lyrics of the song. He sat for fifteen minutes, listened to the radio, and Van Drake's voice cut the music.

"You're good. No one followed you, from the ground or in the sky."

"See you later."

Seven minutes later, JW keyed himself into the apartment, spun his keys on a finger, and lent an eye to the paintings.

"Illisya, baby, I'm here."

"Follow your antenna, hon."

Illisya lay on the bed on her back nude. Two pillows propped her butt six inches from the bed foot, and her drawn legs opened and shut like butterflies' wings.

JW jigged through the bedroom door, gawked on the move, and squatted like a feeding lamb.

Chapter 14

Thunderstorms with massive drops pounded an already miserable Monday afternoon in Miami. Motorists cursed, their chariots skidded, and horns snarled like hounds from Hell. By the displeasure exhibited, none of the sun-loving, hapless populace extended an invitation to the deluge god. Yet the liquid poured like thick fluid sheets, flooding the main thoroughfares into jumbled pileups and gridlocks.

Mary Dawes, other students, and teachers in colorful ponchos and umbrellas waited under the courtyard canopy. The restless children shouted, cried, tramped about, and behaved as terribly as the weather.

Mary rushed from the pen's safety to the gate as a car pulled up. She stepped off from the busy teachers and searched for her Mom at the fringe as the adults ushered kids aboard their parents' vehicles.

A water-soaked rat scampered between the children; they stampeded and screamed louder than the angry auto horns.

"Children, be quiet. It's gone," Mrs. Eisenberg said.

"It was big, wet, and yukky," a child cried.

Mary stomped her impatient feet and braced against the gate. Mrs. Dawes' Rolls approached the curb twenty-one feet away, and an SUV cut in front of it and parked. Horns blasted, and Mrs. Dawes' auto skidded to the far sidewalk on the other side of the pickup area.

Mrs. Dawes reversed. Mary bolted from the pen, and Mrs. Dawes stuck her head out in the downpour.

"Mary, no, wait."

The old, tinted-window, colorless clunker sped down the road and parted the water like Moses' rod at the Red Sea shore. Mary saw movement in her peripheral vision, whipped her head right, stopped, and screamed as the motor roared and accelerated at her.

"Mary. Oh, God, no," Mrs. Dawes cried.

The witnesses screamed, and it resonated like a bunch of tormented souls crying out from an unholy place. The pitchy-patchy blight on wheels slammed into Mary and killed her. Its engine growled, and the tires made waves like a boat as it sped away. Regina screamed and threw her body at Mary's in the knee-deep water. Later, none of the eyewitnesses could describe the car or identify the model to the police.

▲ ▲ ▲

The deluge beat Sad Bum as if it had honored a contract to cleanse him and make him holy. He hunched his shoulders and plodded along in water inches below his knees.

Lightning chopped the sky, and thunder rattled loose teeth in closed mouths across the city.

A car slowed and rolled by the Sad Bum. The red Bentley sped out of the gloom, splashed the Sad Bum from his head down, and braked twenty-five meters away. The Sad Bum brushed grime from his rags; the car door swung open, and he shuffled inside the car.

The Distinguished Gent drove off, and neither acknowledged the other's presence.

Sad Bum dripped water on the leather upholstery, and the song "One Day in the City" blasted on the radio.

"Heroes returned from battles to die in the Streets. Are you, too, a victim in the name of peace? There are no signs on any of these doors. We lived here to work, and change gave no more. Fear is dominant, and trust is gone. It's useless to dream if the dreamer never pursued. One day in the city is a day in the universe. We're miles apart, and we shared the same experiences, for life's a chain of thoughts..."

The lightning cracked like animated things and pulsated to the heavy bass and drums of the music. Eerie shadows danced in both men's eyes as if imprisoned entities behind their pupils fought to escape.

The Distinguished Gent stopped beyond the police caution tape at the scene of Mary's accident and tapped his index finger on the wheel to the beat of the music. Sad Bum goggled at the dashboard, oblivious, as the police operation unfolded.

▲ ▲ ▲

Flooded secondary roads and dirt trails cut the West Kendall wilderness more like tributaries than arteries. The sky, trees, and air mourned in dreary colors as if they witnessed Mary's death and shared the distress in silence. Water poured into a swollen canal, and the killer's automobile skidded close to the bank. Illisya dashed from the unrecognizable Chevy Nova Coupe in an oversized dark hoodie, and incendiary devices blazed inside the clunker. She sprinted and held her hood against her face from the rain. The burnt-out hulk exploded, twisting the metal into grotesque shapes.

She ran two football lengths away and bolted into a thicket. She removed cut limbs from a dirt bike, pushed it onto the road, kick-started it, the motor roared, and she blasted up the road in mud and water with an orb on her head.

▲ ▲ ▲

Visibility on the Rickenbacker Causeway Bridge plunged to feet. Illisya rode behind a truck in the terrible weather. She slowed to a crawl in the middle of the bridge, rode the sidewalk, and dried her helmet. She searched in both directions for headlights, juiced the motorcycle, wheelied, stepped off, and the bike flew over the rails. She tossed her headgear after it, tucked in her shoulders, and scampered back toward the Miami end of the bridge.

Chapter 15

The storm dissipated into light drizzle by nightfall, and Ron ventured out in a T-shirt and shorts, minus one shoe and a sock. He jogged up Meg's driveway and kissed Illisya's car on the dreary, awful night.

Ron stepped back, mindless of the elements, admired the car, and his eyes shone as if he had accomplished a mighty feat. He sighed, pumped a fist, beamed in ecstasy, moved in closer, and peed on the taillights. He glanced at Meg's window, backtracked through puddles of water to his front door, and drew on his other sock and shoe.

▲ ▲ ▲

The full moon hung on the horizon on a long string and shooed dark clouds from its vicinity. Dogs barked in the distance, and the night smelled cleansed and wet. Ron sped up to a footbridge over a canal, hung his head over the rails, and made ugly faces at the moon's reflection on the still water.

His eyes squeezed into intense insanity slits, and he moved like a soldier in action on his toes, and grinned at his reflection. Ron's feverish mind transported him back to his last battle in Afghanistan, and angry tracers buzzed like wasps in vicious crossfires to end all crossfires. Bombs exploded like thunder; shrapnel ripped flesh and metal. A fireball plummeted, and another rose as soldiers shouted until their vocal cords strained to formulate words of fear, bravery, and pain. The frantic voices spat from parched lips in hoarse yells and screams.

A Humvee crashed and threw Ron, and he sprawled on his back in the sand. The clear blue skies called him away from the pain, dust, fire, noise, black smoke, and men at their animalistic lowest point. Injured and dead Marines scattered around him, a woman belched a death scream, and Ron whipped his head to Lacey, trapped in the burning Humvee on its side.

"Lacey."

He tried to get to his feet and crumbled.

"Laccceeey."

Medics dragged him away, and Lacey's Humvee exploded in a fireball.

Back on the footbridge, Ron hopped backward and sang.

"One day in the city is a day in the universe. We're miles apart, and we shared the same experiences. Life is a chain of thoughts. Heroes, returned from battles to die in the Streets."

He jumped on the rail, ran across the bridge like an acrobat, landed, and raced across the Avenue. A car braked, swung, and missed him by its paint.

"Crazy motherfuck, you're lucky. This's my wife's new car and not my truck."

An absentminded Ron sprinted into the small park on NW 179 Street.

▲ ▲ ▲

Deepsy and a scrawny kid named Echo both turned seventeen three weeks back and joined a loose bunch of idiots calling themselves Young Animals two days before. The gang boasted about their initiation acts to new members when they had not even jacked a bag of chips from the corner store.

The day before, the leaders of the Young Hoodlums had asked the two wannabes to burn someone and become life partners. Deepsy and Echo planned to hit someone in the heavy rain in Echo's mother's Florida room. Echo called the gang leader.

"Hey dog, we gonna mix fire with rain over at one-seventy-nine."

"Did you know all the dreads playing soccer strapped?"

Echo hesitated on the line.

"Deepsy, he said the dreads are strapped."

"Tell him we'll work from the other end of the park and to send an observer."

"Yo, I heard him," the leader said.

He hung up the phone.

"We burn anyone who pass through the park tonight," Deepsy said.

Echo slapped Deepsy's hand and bumped chests for their cleverness, for no one would venture through the park on such a fuckup night.

"Neither captains nor majors can blame us now," Deepsy said.

Deepsy lurked in the shadows near the basketball court in the park, half of his hair in dreads and the other side plaited in a ponytail.

His partner held up his oversized pants to his right.

"Do you think they sent someone to watch us?" Echo asked.

"Yeah, but when no one pass through here tonight, they can't say we're soft anymore." Deepsy kissed his rented pistol.

Echo stepped forward, puffed his chest, pumped his right arm back and forth, and freestyled without music.

"Yeah, dawg, for real."

Two rats stood on their hind legs for a moment and dashed under a trash bin.

"I'm gonna slay any motherfuckers that come through here. Bam, bam, bam," Deepsy shouted, hoping the unseen observer heard him.

"Yeah, dog, yeah."

Ron jogged toward the kids, and the boys slunk into the darkness. Deepsy's firearm fell at his side, its muzzle held down, and his thoughts ran amok.

Shit, what's that fool doing out here on a night like this? I've not seen the observer, and Echo may snitch if I back down. Damn, I hope the fool changes direction and runs somewhere else.

Echo tried to read Deepsy's face in the gloom.

Oh my God, I can't back out now, and my Mom is gonna kill me if the cops arrest me.

"The next one is mine, dog," Echo blabbered and slapped his chest to appear brave.

"You know it, dude."

The boys trembled in the dark and wished for a teleportation device to transport them to their warm beds.

What fool runs on such a night? Deepsy asked himself. Even the Jamaicans who played soccer and Ludo night and day in the park stayed home from the weather.

Deepsy wanted to read Echo's body language but didn't want him to see the fear on his face. Fuck, the running fool comes straight at us.

Ron approached yards away. Deepsy broke cover, pointed his weapon sideways, and his hand trembled.

"Punk, you're dead—"

Ron darted to the side, grabbed Deepsy's hand, and broke it.

He pulled the boy to him and broke his neck before he cried, and the ugly sound resonated in the quiet night.

Echo ran; his pants fell around his knees, tripping him. Ron sprang four feet, stomped on the boy's windpipe, crushed it, and blood bubbled from his nostrils.

Ron spun Deepsy's gun on his finger, kissed it, tucked it in his waist, and sang falsetto.

"Heroes returned from battles to die in the Streets. We lived for change, but changes give no more. One day in the city is a day in the universe. We're miles apart, and we share the same experiences. Life's a chain of thoughts."

▲ ▲ ▲

Illisya tucked Meg under her black sheet and adjusted her black pillows, her actions epitomized calmness.

"Girl, you're not so hot tonight. I'm spending the night here," Illisya said.

"Death is not an admirer of hotness. Where's that damn man you're hunting?"

"You'd be shocked at how hard I worked on him."

"A woman like you shouldn't have to work hard to get any man."

Illisya laughed.

"Thanks, but we live in the age of miracles. Everyone's hot. It's like trench warfare these days."

She brushed a lock of hair from Meg's face.

"I've made an important business decision this afternoon, and it should get my heart's desire soon," Illisya said.

Meg closed her eyes, reached out, and touched Illisya's arm.

"I'm happy for you. But who distorted love into a business?"

"King David originated the trend when he sent Uriah to his demise so he could bed his wife. I want you to be around for the marriage. So, take your medication, lest you croak on me."

"Okay, just for the damn nuptials. I've been taking crap from you since you were six damn months old. I'm tired. I wanna leave fucking town."

Illisya wagged her finger at Meg and selected a key from her bunch.

"You know, I wouldn't go into that bright-colored, painted ass room of yours," Meg said.

"Get some sleep."

Illisya sat on a chair, watched Meg doze off, waited another ten minutes, and tiptoed from the room.

▲ ▲ ▲

Illisya opened the door down the hall, slid her hand inside, flicked the light switch, and stood inside the doorway for a minute, still like a statue.

She sucked air into her lungs as she moved to the bed. It creaked as she lay on her back, her arms behind her head, and glued her eyes on JW's clippings-covered wall. The partition to her right contained photos of her and Bill's practiced target shooting in the deep woods, hunting, and roughhousing from age eight.

Illisya sprang off the bed and pulled a black cloth off a shrine built like a four-layer wedding cake with hers and JW's busts as the toppers. She sighed, ripped down everything, and folded them on the bed, one piece at a time.

▲ ▲ ▲

Ron sat on the floor of his room in darkness, his eyes dull and lost somewhere far away. In the background, the song 'One Day In The City' played on his phone. His hand darted for a red candle, and he lit it between his legs.

The candlelight exposed his upper body, painted red, and Deepsy's pistol sat on the floor between his legs. He picked up an old teenage photograph of Illisya and Lacey seated on the red Chevy Nova in Meg's driveway.

He folded the photo into a funnel, stuck it into the gun's muzzle, lit it, and held it an inch from his mad, terror-stricken face.

▲ ▲ ▲

Illisya cracked the back door into Meg's backyard and stepped out into the night with an armful of photographs and newspaper clippings. She dumped them into a burnt drum, darted back into the house, and came out with a bottle of flammable liquid. She cast her eyes into the clear, starry sky as if she mocked the celestials' inquisitive eyes. She squirted the contents onto the drum and set it on fire, her face an emotionless mask.

Chapter 16

Tears fell in every living room in Florida as news of Mary's death saturated the morning programs. The morning sun rejuvenated a bedazzled daybreak in Miami, and police caution tape cordoned off JW's office building's parking lot.

Bereavement permeated the building like an energy-sucking virus. Teary-eyed employees gathered in somber comfort groups, hugged, prayed, and searched their minds for answers when words could not articulate grief.

▲ ▲ ▲

Sergeant Councell worked on Mary Dawes' death until late into the night, and he woke with a grim, overnight state of mind that substance could not dilute. Councell limped past his grouchy wife into the bathroom and recoiled at his shocked early-morning reflection in the mirror. Homefront angst had forced and prepared him to blend into crowds as an insecure being. His wife's countenance grew vicious edges after his late night with her perceived nemesis, his partner Hurtz. However, a child murderer roamed his city byways, and he woke with a job to do. The light in his eyes deflected his domestic troubles into a cold corner for the moment.

Later that morning, officers commandeered two offices as interview rooms. A woman rushed from her chat with Councell and bolted into the restroom.

"Come on in, Mr. Weiss," Councell said.

The senior director spent five minutes with Councell, departed, and crashed into a uniformed officer outside the door, holding a hand over his mouth.

Hours later, the detectives worked singly from the tenth floor up, and Hurtz trailed a distraught Bill to his office. Her eyebrows shot up in approval at Bill's spacious corner office. The child's death sickened her, but she maintained her sweet but complex professional composure.

She tossed a quick, trained eye around, and her expression softened more and more around the edges. Bill sat on his desk, dejected, and his massive shoulders hunched like a folded beach umbrella. Bill's old problems persisted, and he missed the glint of approval in Hurtz's alluring eyes.

"We're in shock. I still can't believe it," Bill said.

"Do you know of anyone who has a grudge against Mr. Dawes?" Hurtz asked.

"No, I don't. Isn't it a hit-and-run accident?" Bill asked.

"It could be anything at this point. I understand you moved into Mr. Dawes' inner circles. Do you know of any jilted former lovers or disgruntled former employees?"

"We haven't fired anyone at this level in years. As for mistresses, I wouldn't know," Bill said.

Hurtz handed Bill her card.

"Call me if you remember anything. Even a minuscule incident can be important," Hurtz said.

Bill nodded, inserted the card into his wallet, sat back on his desk, juggled the wallet, and eyed Detective Hurtz's back as she departed.

He leaned back, closed his eyes, and delved into philosophical rhetoric. How could something so awful happen to such a generous, warm person as JW? Life had taken the best of us after we shared our souls and did our best. Therefore, he proclaimed there were no reasons for karma to repay humanity's gall and other ill experiences for their goodwill.

Why did a fatal mishap not happen to ugly, lying, condescending, racist thieves flaunting their wares in Congress and on TV? Unscrupulous people recovered from the killer virus, yet his friend Valrie and his brother Blemo died from it. He loved Illisya since childhood and only enjoyed her peeks and taunts as a result. His feelings for her bulldozed other women out of the way. He desperately wanted to hold on to a girlfriend for more than a month.

He traveled far along unknown worlds. Why did a terrible cataclysm never happen to people like Illisya? He asked himself how low the sun must drop over South Florida before he admitted his chances with her were nil. Yes, he hoped and wished a monster rose from Biscayne Bay and gobbled up her non-fucking ass. Yes, he finally said it. Bill had reached the stage of the man who begged his wife to come back home day after day, and one morning, as he picked up the phone, he got an epiphany. Instead of debasing himself over her, why didn't he purge his heart of her love?

Bill smiled from his soul for the first time in a year and tried to arrest a further drift into the fox-and-sour-grapes den. His mind opened to a hard-as-stone fact. He wished ill will on Illisya for the first time, and it felt good.

He should do it again and shout it too.

"Illisya, I hoped your ship sailed, hit monsters in the mist, and sank."

Bill slammed a fist into his palm.

"It's time for the man in me to step out into the evil world and strive, and I aim to participate in what's out there," Bill lamented, and made plans to party with the island women dancing in the artwork on the wall.

"I wanna dance with you all somewhere in the sun. And fuck the non-fucking beautiful, evil witch. I hope the worst disaster happens to her. The type that'll send her to the hospital to suffer for months or worse."

His eyes bulged, a wild expression took over his face, his body trembled, and he glanced around the office, grinning.

"I sanctified my system. In fact, I hate the fuck outta you, Illisya Haynes, and your killer Papa, from this minute forward. I hope he rotted somewhere nasty, and you join him soon."

Bill gawked, surprised at his quiet outburst. If he could see the expression on his face, he would run. He tossed his wallet on the desk and stormed out of his office, angry as the lion, the monkey smacked with a stone while it slept.

▲ ▲ ▲

Hurtz and Councell exited JW's building, and a late evening sun blazed a trail from the ferry to JW's mansion. The officers entered the mansion through a beautiful Victoria Stiffkey blue-painted door.

"Sir, I'm Detective Hurtz, and this is my partner, Sgt. Councell."

"We extend our sincere condolences to you and your wife on behalf of the department, Mr. Dawes," Councell said.

JW stuck out a lifeless arm, and Hurtz shook it.

"Come on inside."

JW wheeled away, and the detectives followed the haggard man into his downstairs study. He tumbled into a chair under the influence of grief and mental fatigue, like someone who planned never to rise and live again.

"Do you have any idea, Mr. Dawes, who could've killed your daughter?" Hurtz asked.

"Are you certain it wasn't some drunken kid?" JW asked.

"We have to look at every angle," Councell said.

"I can't believe someone would murder my little girl. I can't..." Tears streamed down JW's cheeks.

"It's a cluttered board at this time, sir," Hurtz said.

"These are routine questions, sir," Councell assured.

"Have you received any anonymous phone calls or threats?" Hurtz asked.

"Oh, no, my security people would be all over it."

"How's Mrs. Dawes holding up?" Hurtz asked.

"Our doctor sedated her and is with her."

"We'll need a statement from her as soon as she's up to it," Councell said.

"I'm certain she'll be glad to help when she's capable. Did you glean anything from the eyewitnesses?" JW asked.

"No, other than everyone agreeing it was an old dirt-gray, dark-windows car, not much," Hurtz said.

JW's head fell onto his desk.

"We have no further questions currently, Mr. Dawes. We'll let ourselves out," Hurtz said. Hurtz swore under her breath that she never wanted to see another person suffer such mental distress as a wounded JW Dawes.

Chapter 17

At 8:13 a.m., Illisya searched Meg's cupboards in her pajamas and moved to the refrigerator.

"What are you searching for in there?" Meg called.

"Something to cook for breakfast."

"Haul your ass down to one of those pancake places, get me a stack with butter, and slash the syrup."

"No, she didn't speak to me like her stepchild."

"Look here..."

"I'm twenty-six and done it four times, and that is more than you at ninety-five."

"Kiss my butt."

Illisya grinned.

"I'll be right back, queenie."

"When you return, pull cerassee off the fence and draw some strong tea for me."

"How does that bitter brew and pancakes work?"

"My guess is you'll never know."

On her way back, Illisya purchased a *Miami Herald* newspaper the morning after she murdered Mary.

▲ ▲ ▲

Later in the afternoon, Kali dug into a garden salad from a window table at Rose, their favorite café. An amused Illisya broke a breadstick, tried to block the hubbub interactions of the other patrons, and settled cozily into their world.

"How can I change your mind?" Kali asked.

"It's too late now. I got my place."

Kali hung her head, dejected.

"I thought you were at Meg's for the last two nights?"

"Yes, she was ill."

"Damn, I guess my screaming finally did it. When poked at one end, free-willed people express pleasure through the other."

Kali widened her eyes at Illisya's silly grin.

"Oh, and I swore you did it on purpose to aggravate me because of my virgin status."

"Oh, no, it's naturally ingrained. Hey, wait one fucking minute here."

Kali's eyes grew expansive as the eastern ocean on a cloudless morning, and she swallowed two yellow pills. Illisya grinned at her reaction and sipped her drink.

"You kept things from me. Damn, you know how dysfunctional I already am."

Kali shook her head and jabbed her finger. Illisya wiped her mouth and smirked.

"Hush, I sailed through four times to get the dust off the road," Illisya said.

"People cruise through the fucking Panama Canal, Illisya?"

Kali sank half a glass of wine.

"So, who tore you up? Tell me about it."

"I instructed him to rip and almost pass out from the fucking pain the first time."

"The steel maiden ass syndrome is gonna kill you."

"I made a first impressive point to last forever, and I learned something else too. A dick and one's finger are not the same," Illisya said.

"I could've told you as much and saved you the trouble of shredding your butt to make a point."

Illisya glowed as she relished the moment again. Kali frowned at her and everything else near Jupiter and God's front door.

"Over the years, I came to realize we're freaks, weird, and crazy alike," Kali said.

"Friends do have to share some common ground."

"Let's drink to common ground," Kali said.

They picked up their glasses and knocked them together.

"To friendship, common ground, and unbroken hearts."

"To friendship, common ground, and unbroken hearts."

Kali popped a red pill, emptied her glass, and dabbed at her mouth. Illisya sipped water and smirked. Kali tried to read the mysterious shrewdness in her eyes and hit the same old wall. She could never fathom Illisya's eyes or tell if they suffered from tiredness or intended to commit mayhem. The murder part came into play after she slew Jack O'Spade last year.

I understood, Illisya, but I was so wrong. Where's Dread? I need him, and it itched deep.

"You'll have to find a new roommate or move back to your mom's place," Illisya said.

Kali cleared the fog from her head, but bitterness resurfaced, crawled all over her system, and settled on her face.

"I'm going home, alright."

"Are you?"

"Yes, it's written."

"You have my full support," Illisya said.

Kali poured grief and sorrow onto the table.

"My whole life has been a spectacle, like I'm outside myself, and I discern from an empty, foggy place at a distance away."

Kali wiped tears from her eyes.

"I arrived in this world innocent, and my racist ass mom corrupted me."

Kali's body shook, and Illisya hugged her across the table.

"She molded me into a monster. Please forgive me for being a horrible person."

"If parents knew best, the world would've been a wonderful place to live. Don't you think?" Illisya asked.

"It's so terrible when your parents are your first enemy. They inhibited my mental growth, clouded my perspectives, and plain fucked up my head."

Kali buried her face on Illisya's shoulder.

"It takes four years of therapy to make me see the clear blue sky. Now it's payback time."

"Do you see forgiveness anywhere on your horizon?" Illisya asked.

"How can I forgive the incorrigible? Am I the local saint?"

"Digging deep would help."

"Bitch, you're all business, business, and more business. You're no Dr. Jill."

Illisya hugged Kali, and her frigid eyes glared over her shoulder at things dubious and soon to happen.

"I've got to run," Kali said.

"Dread again?"

"In times like these, I need my medication," Kali said.

They pecked each other's cheeks, and Kali thought of hot afternoon sex, motored out of the café light as an Elysian feather. Illisya's eyes followed her, and she shook her head in wonderment.

"In a few more months, the poor skinny boy gonna be worn out at the peak of his life."

Kali's car squealed out of the parking lot, and an unmarked car followed her. An amused Illisya's eyes glinted and formed two slits. The conversations buzzing in the restaurant caught up to Illisya. Patrons babbled not about politics or the usual sports games, but about poor little dead Mary, and it riled her. She wanted to ask them if they realized how thousands of children died in hellholes per minute. Does the world care about anyone not within arm's reach or earshot? Brainwashed sheepies allowed their leaders to create wars and conflicts, and when one of the other suckers killed one of their soldiers, their hands and voices flew up in righteous indignation as if the other fucking jocks held dicks instead of rifles.

Things have changed while you all slept. Brain-eating braggadocio entities run the world these days. Check who you voted for and ask yourself how only someone evil could kill such a sweet, innocent girl. What do you think wars have been doing? Define innocence, or who or what is pure for a moment. When did the sins of ancestors refuse to shadow the succeeding generations? Motherfuckers worked their brain cells to cinders to make the words fulfilled.

Illisya sneered at the world, held a hand up, and signaled for her check.

"Rivers have to run dry at times, for the so-called word to pass."

She glared at the patrons around her and out the window at the sunshiny, innocent day.

"It would've been a dull world without urban hunter-gatherers like me," Illisya continued.

She smiled at the new job description she coined, spilled sweetness at the waiter, and left a fifty-dollar tip.

She picked up the police tail on Kali months ago and worked it into her scheme. If the law wanted something to do, she planned to give it to them. They still followed Kali around like a puppy dog, and she hoped they didn't sniff around her butt for too long, ahead of schedule. She felt empowered, like someone who held the narrative in every line and movement on the stage.

"Officers, I'm the audience, the actors, the stagehands, and the directors in my little drama as it unfolds," Illisya mumbled.

Chapter 18

On the second day after the murder, Carlos drove his old pickup truck to his fishing hole and tapped the wheel to the reggaeton remix of "One Day in the City" on his radio.' He sang the hook off-key, drove around a corner, and braked six feet from Illisya's burnt-out car in the trail. Carlos dialed 911.

Within an hour, police and news helicopters circled above the wreckage while ground vehicles and personnel saturated the area. Councell directed the operation as they hoisted the car onto a wrecker.

At midday, Councell and Hurtz hovered over two evidence techs as they dissected the burnt-out husk in the MPD evidence garage. The men removed the transmission and placed it on a mat.

"If they did work on the box. We may find a print," tech one said.

"Thanks. I'll check back with you later," Councell said.

Hurtz hovered over the counter, and the tech gave her a trespasser's glare. She tossed her surgical gloves into the trash and followed Councell out.

▲ ▲ ▲

At 9:00 p.m., two nights after Mary's death, JW's office building stood cold, quiet, and empty as if it suppressed the fear of an evil, cruel fate. Bill Kelly, a habitual late worker, stood, worn and distraught, at his office window, gazing at the city lights. He sighed, reached for his bag, flicked the light off, and slammed the office door on his way out. A shadowy figure scuttled into a utility closet down the hall as the sound of the door reverberated through the building.

Bill glanced over his shoulders twice as if he sensed a presence at the elevator, turned his head, and peeked down the hallway as he boarded the lift.

A preoccupied and devastated Bill strolled to his car in the empty lot; the warm, cloudy night drooped his shoulders onto his knees. He wore the weight of the killing as a permanent burden and missed a rat as it dashed across his path. Bill froze as if jolted, slapped his pocket for his wallet, and backtracked into the building. The lone security officer lingered around the reception desk as Bill keyed himself back inside.

"I left my wallet on my desk for the second evening. What an awful night," Bill said.

"These are crazy times, sir."

"How can it be muggy as Hell and cloudy at the same time?" Bill asked.

"It's going to rain. I mean pour."

"I'll never love the rain again."

He disappeared into the elevator.

▲ ▲ ▲

Illisya exited the closet with a heavy backpack and picked the lock on Bill's office. She stooped under Bill's desk, removed electronic bugs, and sat on his desk. Bill's wallet pressed into her backside, and she pushed it away from her.

She heard the thump of heavy footsteps tramping down the hall; she grabbed her bag and squeezed behind a file cabinet in a nook. Bill barged inside, retrieved Hurtz's card from his wallet, and dialed.

"How did I forget?" Bill mumbled.

"You've reached Detective Hurtz."

"Bill Kelly here, Detective. I remember something, but it's probably nothing—"

"Where are you, Mr. Kelly?"

"I'm in my office."

"I'm just four blocks away. Do you mind?" Hurtz asked.

"Not at all, ma'am."

"You can call me Karolina."

"I like that, Karolina. I'll inform security you're on your way up."

Bill hung up and pondered. What happened between JW and Illisya the night he introduced them at the party? He heard she came to the office seeking a job or money for an investment project. Illisya and an investment project, huh? What the Hell had she placed on the fire? He wouldn't call her a thief; he gave her that much. However, it wouldn't surprise him if she sought money to reinvent Amazon. She possessed the gumption to do anything and invested her energies in a dark, secret project somewhere for years.

His desk phone rang, and he punched the speaker button.

"The officer is here, sir."

"Very well. I'll meet her at the elevator."

Hurtz said goodbye to Councell earlier as he prepared to leave the office for his North Miami home. She deliberated about a beer or two at her favorite bar. However, another animalistic predator's urge compelled her to drive by the Dawes building. Big Bill Kelly impressed her, and she hoped she might run into him. What began as a playful sand-grain idea grew into a wet ocean as she approached JW's office block. If she caught any sign of life, she would ask for Bill on official business and see where it led.

Hurtz cruised four blocks from Bill's office in a mellow mood, anticipating personal, sensual possibilities in an encounter with the giant. The phone rang, startled her, and Bill croaked in her ear.

Illisya peeked out at Bill as he left the office and ducked her head as he escorted Hurtz back. Bill's arms elaborated as he escorted Hurtz to a chair and sat at his desk. Experience told Illisya he reached a state of high excitement and shared his information with the Detective.

"I introduced them at the party. I've no idea what transpired after or if it means anything. However, Illisya obsessed herself over someone from age seventeen, if I recall correctly, and minutes ago it hit me. It's gotta be JW," Bill continued.

"Do you know where we can contact Miss Haynes?" Hurtz asked.

"I can call her to meet me somewhere."

"Yes, we have some questions we'd like to ask her."

Illisya leaped from behind the file cabinet and pointed a gun at Hurtz. Bill peered into the dark maw of the silencer in her gloved hands and saw his demise gaze back at him. Bill and Illisya's target practice at the range and in the wild, her accuracy with firearms, scared him to death.

"Here I am. Who wants to ask me questions?" Illisya asked.

Hurtz attempted to reach for her gun, and Illisya covered her as Bill froze in his chair.

"I always knew you were a rat, Billy Boy."

Hurtz flinched.

"I wouldn't do that, officer," Illisya said.

"You don't want to do this. You're in enough trouble as it is already," Hurtz said.

"Shut up and slowly remove your gun and slide it over."

Hurtz complied. Illisya picked up the gun and pointed both firearms at them. Although under a gun, Hurtz couldn't help but recall her and Councell's conversation concerning Illisya in the café's parking lot. She would pat herself on the back for being an excellent character reader if she could only twitch under the evil beauty's guns.

"Please push the chair away from the desk, Detective, and may I have your backup piece, ma'am?" Illisya growled.

Hurtz hesitated. Illisya shot the chair foot off, and Hurtz sprawled onto the carpet on her backside.

"May I now have your backup piece, please?"

Hurtz tried to get to her feet.

"No, no, no. Do it from down there and slide it over."

Hurtz slid the gun, and Illisya kicked it away.

"Pull her pants down, Bill."

"Hell no."

"Do it or die, Bill," Illisya barked.

Illisya scared him to death when she called him Bill twice. In the past, she had only called him Bill when she was ultra-furious. He once invaded her privacy in a river in the woods, and she caught him.

"Billy Boy, go away. I'm not giving it up."

Later, around the campfire, he couldn't meet her eyes. The fact that she caught him deflated and shamed him far beyond the transgression. But she cheered Bill up and joked about it.

"Billy Boy, only a wuss wouldn't try to see where I kept my treasure," she said.

Days later, behind Mr. Haynes, she commanded Bill to sit on a rock while she skinny-dipped. To hide his embarrassment, Bill waited fifteen minutes after she left and crawled into the chilly water. But now she called him Bill and pointed two guns at his face.

Ice formed around Bill's heart and squeezed his arteries, for Illisya, the daughter of one killer named Haynes, held two guns on him.

"Do it, Bill."

She poked him with a gun, and a reluctant Bill bent over Hurtz.

"Don't do it," Hurtz said.

"Detective, it would be wise to keep your mouth closed. Continue, Bill," Illisya barked.

One day, at eighteen, Bill's moxie overpowered his good sense, and he handled her business intentionally during a training exercise.

"Billy Boy, your head gets fuzzy when you don't see digits and charts to crunch but try not to do it again."

Fuck, she called me Bill again. He felt painted into an ugly corner, with two guns pointed at his head, held in hands steady as high-rise columns.

Bill exhaled a gust of wind, fumbled with Hurtz's belt buckle, and it stuck. He suspected she flexed her stomach.

Illisya's black yoga pants burned a permanent place in Bill's brain. Who the fuck wore yoga pants to slay people? Did she know what it took to restrain himself seeing her in yoga pants? Bill felt ashamed thinking about her like that because he had hated her ass since yesterday.

"Pull and toss everything she's wearing," Illisya snapped.

Illisya's sharp command jolted Bill back from dreamland as Hurtz squirmed and locked her legs. Illisya pointed her gun at the officer's face and kicked Bill in the butt.

"What's the meaning of this?" Hurtz demanded.

Hurtz shuffled, and Illisya kicked her in the face.

"Are we turning this into a Q and A session? Bill, get down on her. That's what she came for anyway. She could've taken the info over the phone."

"Sick shit. I'll not do it," Bill snapped.

Illisya poked Bill.

"Get down on your knees. You didn't complain when I blew you."

Bill dropped to his knees.

"Please don't make me do this, Illisya."

Illisya's military boot pressed into his back, and the gun stiffened over Hurtz's face.

"Did I complain when I paid you on my knees for JW's introduction?" Illisya asked.

Hurtz tried to close her legs.

"Oh my God. She's gonna kill us," Hurtz blurted.

Bill turned his head to tackle Illisya, and she calmly shot him through the side of his head mid-turn. Hurtz screamed, and Illisya shot her twice in the face and threw the guns on top of the bodies.

She frowned down at Bill's body.

"I warned you about the dangers of working too late several times, Billy Boy."

She dug for his phone, de-cloned it, replaced it in his pocket, pulled her bag from behind the file cabinet, and sat on the desk.

▲ ▲ ▲

It went from a warm night on a nickel to a rainy, miserable, foggy, wet one. No one should drive in it, much less trudge through the slush on foot. The angry night threw in lightning and struck the ominous clouds every few seconds for effect.

A robust woman cringed under a bus shelter on Biscayne Avenue as the electric storm crisscrossed the sky.

Lightning struck five people under a bus shelter a week back, and the news ran the incident for one year in a single week.

"At my size, a bolt couldn't miss me if it came visiting the shelter," she mumbled.

She squeezed against the corner as a skinny man in a sharp suit ran under the shed, fighting his umbrella.

He couldn't take the brunt of a bolt and save me at his size. But he could at least start a conversation and keep my mind off fiery death bolts.

"Hi," the man said.

He brushed water off his fedora and sneaked an eye at the woman.

"Hello there, sir."

His island accent came over thick to her, and it was hard to tell when he arrived. The skinny Jamaican she married lived in Fort Lauderdale for thirty years, and he held on to his accent like a piece of his soul. She had experienced the island men's love for full-bodied women. However, her Green Card machine ran out of service and would not reopen unless the authorities found a way to chain the next man she married to her forever.

The heavy-set woman and the skinny man indulged in deep conversations and waved their arms to rival Kali, the goddess.

A potbellied man, Mr. Dofus, ran under the shed and stood at the other end of the shelter. The heavy-set woman figured him for about forty-five, but he ran much faster and lighter for his size. What people called being nosy, she called being observant.

A city bus rolled up, and Mr. Dofus boarded first.

"You can call me, but if you're after that Green Card, don't bother," the woman said.

"Green wasn't the color I'm after."

"What color are you after, my friend?"

"Oh, something in the reddish-pink department."

She placed one foot on the bus steps and fished in her pocketbook for change.

"Oh, call me soon. I've red-pink acres of them all."

She smiled at the man and disappeared inside the bus.

She liked her cards served face up. Mr. Skinny wanted to nail her, and she didn't mind one bit. It's savagery by mutual consent, as the reggae song said. She gawked at him through the window and wondered if he danced dirty Dancehall music on a fatty bum-bum.

▲ ▲ ▲

At 10:00 p.m., the temperature inside the JW Dawes building dropped, and the security man hauled on his jacket and walked his rounds. He rode the elevator to the top floor and descended the stairs to kill boredom. The last cleaner left at 7:45 p.m., and Bill Kelly left at 8:30 p.m. and returned at 8:36 p.m.

"Wait, the cop arrived at 8:41 p.m. What're they doing up there?"

He glanced at his chart and wristwatch as he exited the eleventh floor and headed for the fire escape.

"I'm gonna knock them up and tell them the building is my domain at night. They should find a hotel."

The security man reported the crime at 10:30 p.m. Councell's phone rang five minutes later as he pulled into his driveway.

"Hello."

"Something terrible happened to Detective Hurtz."

"What are you saying? I spoke to her not too long ago."

"Someone shot her in JW Dawes' building about two hours ago, sir."

The shocking news numbed his brain for a minute, and the phone fell from his hand. He sat at the car controls, dazed, and in his stupor, he glimpsed his wife's silhouette at the living room window, gazing out at the vehicle. Councell's appalled brain refused to function as the seconds ticked. Notwithstanding the death of his partner, someone murdered a person whom he cared for and had a profound respect for on and off the job. He shamefully admitted that the horrible news gave him a lifeline to retreat from a toxic home environment.

Councell broke the conflicted chain of thought, woke from the haze, backed out of the driveway, and blasted away. He flicked his emergency dashboard lights on as his cell phone rang two hundred yards from his house, and he answered it.

"They found Hurtz shot to death. I got the news while I sat in the driveway."

The silence dragged on for long seconds, and he eyed the phone on the stand.

"I'm sorry to hear. Please be careful out there," Mrs. Peggy Sue Councell said.

"Thanks, it's gonna be a long night."

He cut the call, and a million distressful thoughts ran back and forth through his head.

Suppose my wife killed her? She was so jealous of us working together.

Mrs. Peggy Sue Councell, a beautiful thirty-six-year-old woman, never beheld her outer beauty. The image that stared back at her in the mirror differed from the one the world glimpsed, and she hated the version she saw daily. Well-wishers hinted and nudged her toward therapy for her insecurity from her college years. Still, she made excuses and never sought the help she needed. The young beauty grew into a troubled woman and struggled through life burdened under an invisible load up the slopes of Mount Everest. Peggy Sue copied her mother's behavioral formulas and never grasped her problems by the handle.

My mom lived a happy life, smiled on rare occasions, and I endorsed her mantra. It served her well, and it's good enough for me, she convinced herself.

Peggy Sue stood in the master bedroom doorway and gripped her phone as if she wanted to crush it. She slept in the guest room, not in her husband's bed, for 18 months. Peggy Sue stepped into the master bedroom, her movements sure-footed and robust, stripped to her undies, climbed on the bed, and curled on her side.

She said a silent prayer to the Lord:

I carried no rancor in my heart for Officer Hurtz. Nonetheless, a woman as beautiful as her shouldn't ride around in the dead of night in an automobile with my husband. My mother called it an unnatural thing for him to do from her deathbed. God, please bless her precious soul. My husband could've gotten a male partner, but he kept the beautiful woman as his sidekick for eighteen months. My man asked me night and day why I slept in the locked guest room as if he expected me to tell him how he must conduct himself at work to enhance his home affairs. Some kind of detective, my husband turned out to be. My condolences go out to the Hurtz family, and Lord, I pray for the peaceful transition of her soul. However, I'm back in my husband's bed, where I belong, and I'll remain here until he walks in on me in my glory. My presence will purge the bitter, corroded edge of his soul, invigorate his mind, and lead him to what he needs to do. Thank you, Lord, for listening to me tonight, Amen.

Peggy Sue unpinned her bras, tossed them in the doorway, pulled off her panties, wheeled them on an index finger, threw them beside her bras, gathered the covers up to her chin, and beamed.

"I've patience, and he's coming back here before my sweet Lord Jesus returns."

▲ ▲ ▲

Councell rushed into the Dawes building and caught Blundell, a young detective, questioning the security officer. The grim-faced officers at the scene cleared a path, and he approached the late Bill Kelly's office. Det. Councell stood a foot from the covered bodies, and his brain acted like a camera as he deciphered the crime scene. The shot-off chair leg told him that the perpetrator or perpetrators had ambushed Hurtz in the chair and forced her to disarm herself. He made a three-sixty and withdrew from the murder scene after five minutes without speaking a word.

Chapter 19

A stern-faced AI tech uploaded a thumb and an index fingerprint into her computer's Automated Fingerprint Identification System in the Miami-Dade crime lab. She yawned as faces ran on the screen and settled on former Marine Lacey Gibson.

"Fuck."

At 2:00 a.m., she dialed an inter-office number and passed on her find.

Fifteen minutes later, Councell briefed grim-visaged officers, and he didn't have to remind anyone that a dear member of theirs lay dead in the morgue.

"So far, we found the fingerprint of a Marine who died in Iraq inside the alleged hit-and-run car transmission."

Councell handed out files.

"Blundell, you're with me."

Blundell cherished the opportunity to work with the legendary Councell as his wingman. He wanted to celebrate, but he maintained his professional composure. Not every day did they call out twenty-six-year-old rookies on such a critical case alongside the department's best. His self-confidence grew, and rivers of juice flowed to the right places. He regretted Detective Hurtz's demise, which aided his upward mobility. She was a shrewd investigator and showed respect whenever she spoke to those of lower rank, including himself and others.

"I'm especially interested in the connection between Bill Kelly and the former Marine. Our sister went down in the line of duty. Get me someone to hurt," Councell said.

The officers filed out of the room, and Blundell approached Councell.

"What a sorry mess," Councell said.

"Do you believe it's connected to the kid's death, sir?"

"Without a fucking doubt, and we're gonna hunt down every missing particle and connect them."

"I'm gonna start on traffic, ATMs, and CCTV cameras in the area of the Dawes building," Blundell said.

"Yes, I want footage from all cams going to and from the crime scene checked."

"It rained all night, and the visibility dipped," Blundell said.

"Captain Gonzales will loan you twenty-five uniforms to help expedite the cams."

"Great, Sarge."

Blundell bolted through the door, and Councell labored into the chair at his desk. He sank two cans of energy drinks, picked up the desk phone, and replaced it.

The last call Hurtz received came from Bill Kelly, and minutes later, they lay dead. If the perp or perps followed Hurtz, they would've killed the lone security man in the lobby. The building has no other entrances, and the back exit opens from inside the ground floor. CCTV showed no one entered or left through the door other than Kelly and Hurtz at the time.

I surmised Kelly and Hurtz walked in on the killer in his office. Did he remove or place something in Kelly's office? Security said Kelly left the building at 8:30 p.m. and returned alone six minutes later. He believed someone entered Bill Kelly's office after he departed, and Kelly caught the suspect off guard when he returned. The villain could've stayed hidden, avoided confrontation, and waited them out. Why did he or they never slay Kelly and escape long before Hurtz got there?

He slapped his head. Of course, he waited to hear what Bill had to say to Hurtz. Kelly named the murderer to Hurtz as a person of interest, and the suspect could be someone close to Bill, the office, or JW Dawes. Yes, someone Bill Kelly knew shot him and Hurtz. Intimate knowledge of the case ultimately led to their demise.

"I must revisit Dawes and check Bill Kelly's clients and associates for alibis."

Councell held his phone and paced around his desk as Blundell returned to the office.

"Am I a smoker or a nonsmoker?" Councell asked.

He slapped his coat pockets.

I need a second breath because I may have to tear down the pedestal I built for my boss, Blundell surmised.

Blundell opened his mouth to speak and thought better of it.

"Someone entered the building during the day and never left until after the murders. We've got a line on our killer when we identified the unwanted stayover guest," Councell said.

"I'm on it, sir," Blundell answered, surprised his boss saw him, for Councell faced away from the open door.

At 10:15 a.m., Blundell returned to Councell's office with a file.

"Boss, this is what we have so far."

He handed the folder to Councell, and by the weight of it, he figured it carried no significant findings.

"Four cleaners from a local cleaning service entered the building at 6:00 p.m., and the interior CCTV system went down at 6:30 p.m.," Blundell said.

"Fuck. What gender?"

"Two of each. However, none of the four knew when the others left. Each cleaner finished their job and left for other assignments."

"What did the security man have to say?" Councell asked.

"He didn't pay much attention to a nightly routine, sir."

"Son, we've got a professional lowlife on our hands."

Det. Sergeant Councell stood and exhaled, and a chill ran through his body.

"I don't think he planned the murders. Billy Kelly set off his death by calling Hurtz with information while the bad guy lurked either in the office or listened via a bug," Councell said.

"But why kill an officer?"

"Bill met Hurtz at the elevator and walked her to the office," Councell said.

"Fuck, he dropped the killer's name."

"And did so again in his office, I bet. Check Bill's office for electronic bugs ASAP."

"I'm on it, sir," Blundell said.

Blundell rushed from the room, and Councell coughed into his elbow. The lack of sleep began to bite him in unusual places.

Chapter 20

By 10:00 a.m., the morning after Bill and Hurtz's killing, Miami Roads dried like a desert with no sign of the night's showers. Allman tucked away his funeral home on SW 13th Street off Brickell Avenue as if he hid it from prying eyes. The structure resembled the result of an upscale church caught seducing an emporium.

A disheveled JW hurried from his chauffeur-driven car, flanked by Van Drake, and bolted through a side door. Mr. Allman, the owner of an academic face, met JW in a red-carpeted foyer. For sixty years, Mr. Allman tried to appear somber and businesslike at profound moments, but as usual, he failed. JW accompanied his Dad on business trips to visit Mr. Allman, and it amused him how the mortician tried to change his expression from morbid to businesslike. When the elder Dawes died, JW joked with Regina that Mr. Allman sold the wiry into weary without trying. The status quo remained permanent. Mr. Allman disposed of bodies for the late Mr. Dawes, and a forced trip to hell couldn't wrinkle his everyday black suit. Mr. Dawes instructed JW to retain Mr. Allman because he might need his services at any time.

The two men shook hands.

"JW, words cannot convey my grief to you and your wife."

JW held onto his hand for a moment for strength.

"Thank you, Mr. Allman."

"I must ask if you're ready to make funeral arrangements?"

"The word funeral sounds so agonizing and final. Nevertheless, as distasteful as I find it, that's one of my reasons for visiting you."

Mr. Allman ushered JW into his office and closed the door. They emerged after twenty-five minutes.

"Do you have a private office with a secure telephone?" JW asked.

"But of course, JW."

Mr. Allman led him down the hall, into a soundproof office, and closed the door. JW's security man assumed position outside.

JW paced back and forth with the phone close to his ear in the windowless space as it rang on the other end.

Illisya relaxed on her sofa, feet up, and answered JW's call.

"Oh, my God, hon, Mary didn't die alone. I practically died when I heard the news, even though I didn't know her. Who could've done such a terrible thing?" Illisya asked.

JW's sad face reflected his tortured soul in the drab gray room.

"Did you watch the news today?" JW asked.

Illisya posed the epitome of calmness.

"No, baby, I'm feeling more like running, but the sky is too expansive."

The murders of Mary, Bill, and Hurtz overwhelmed JW, and he cried. His tears flowed as if they came from an offshoot of a river in the rainy season.

"They found Bill Kelly and Detective Hurtz murdered in his office last night," JW said.

Illisya wiggled for a sweet spot. A cloud of unemotional façade zipped over her face.

"Oh, my God, no, not Bill. How could something so awful happen? Bill and I went to kindergarten together. How did he die?"

She bawled into the phone. JW cringed at every sob as if he received punches in his gut against a wall.

"Someone shot them, and the cops are not saying much about the details."

"Hon, what are you going to do?" Illisya asked.

JW leaned against the wall.

"I left Regina a total wreck. She's unable to conceive again, you know."

Illisya smiled.

"My God, it got more terrible by the minute. I can't imagine what she's going through, hon. I felt an excruciating pain in my gut for her," Illisya said.

JW wiped his tears.

"Illisya, what kind of sick motherfucker could've, could've...?"

Illisya sat upright, her knees drawn, her face expressionless.

"The world's full of crazy sick people, baby. What is the law doing?" Illisya asked.

JW changed the phone from his right ear to his left.

"They've half the force working the case now," JW said.

Illisya worked her legs over the back of the couch wing as if she felt needles in them.

"Baby, it's just a matter of hours before the police bring them to justice."

JW perched on the desk and got right back up.

"I, I, I don't know what to do, Illisya."

Illisya dropped her free hand between her legs.

"I'll be praying for you and Regina."

JW stood upright and dabbed at his eyes.

"I must conclude business here and get back to Regina. I'm so sorry to have bothered you."

Illisya adjusted the cushion under her head.

"I wouldn't have forgiven you if you didn't. Remember to be strong for Regina, babes. She needs you now more than ever."

"I'll talk to you when I can, Illisya."

"Please, go to her, babes. I'm here when you need me. Oh, God, poor Bill."

JW hung up. Illisya closed her eyes, and her face remained flexible like a mossy rock in a cold stream.

▲ ▲ ▲

Councell's red-eyed, long-faced team gathered in the briefing room at MPD, and Blundell took the floor.

"Marine Gibson turned in her plates a week before she deployed. There are no other records of the car. She maintained the car through high school herself."

"Please don't tell me someone planned these murders years ago?" Councell asked.

"Detective Hurtz found herself in the wrong place at the wrong time, I think."

"Bill and the Gibson girl went to Central High, but we can't find anyone who saw those two cross paths," an officer said.

"The connection will rip this case open, and my gut tells me it's not over yet," Councell said.

"Both Dawes and his wife's phone records are clean," Blundell said.

"What about the mistresses' angle?"

"So far, nothing, and Dawes' security people tailed our people for tailing them," Blundell said.

"Van Drake's doing, I bet. JW is too clean, and the sky is not that blue," Councell said.

"Should I send Wilson and Konta down to the VA Hospital to interview Ron Gibson?" Blundell asked.

"Nothing he says is admissible. However, you can never tell where a gem may lead."

"It couldn't hurt at this point," Blundell said.

"Are there any questions?" Councell asked.

The stern-faced men and women shook their heads. They'd lost one of theirs, and the fraternity needed bones to chew.

▲ ▲ ▲

A meticulous Councell leafed through the files on his desk, took the discarded ones to the shredder, re-examined them, and fed them into the machine. He appeared more determined than tired for a man who toiled through the night and well into the day. As another long night approached, he analyzed every angle of the reports brought to his desk.

The hero cop in the movies always has a cranky wife whose mom taught her that cherries came from apple trees. She bundled the kids and ran to an aunt or sister in Timbuktu if someone told her otherwise. The Dawes case could break a marriage, even one that masqueraded through each month and stood ready to activate the charade before the new month began.

The facts of engagements eluded Hollywood writers for decades. Heroes are not mere humans. They're dedicated exterminators and operators of machinery that fix time so Tom and Jane can find a semblance of happiness. We, the designated, do not take our roles like ball games or nine-to-five gigs. Police officers throw themselves into their endeavors and don't drown their asses in bottles when chilly winds blow in their faces.

"But does my wife get it or ever will?"

The last time he spoke to God, the Almighty didn't think Peggy Sue would grasp an inevitable reality in her present dispensation. Still, as an optimist, he went home, faced the coldness of his wife, took a shower, changed his clothes, or went to bed in the icy atmosphere.

Did those scribes check the timeline to see what transpired when heroes rotted away on bottles? The next time you see them, explain how the disrupters of decency of time came out and played terrible evil games while the heroes were indisposed on bottles.

The second progress report came at noon, and Councell glanced at his watch. He barely had enough time to go home, shower, and change clothes. The bitch of a case was going to play long and zigzag like one of Hurtz's toothache-type arguments. God bless her soul.

He logged out of his computer and reached for his coat from the chair's back.

Det. Councell returned to the station two hours after the briefing should have begun. He glowed like he'd found Hurtz and the Dawes kid alive inside his car. The squad knew his wife had released him from the abyss into sunny bliss, and he indulged until it hurt. However, they toiled to get him up to speed on the minute details gleaned from the two cases combined.

Chapter 21

High-tech gadgets and appliance lights blinked on and off like lonely entities, calling for human attention from their cold, dead location inside the Dawes' mansion. Since Mary's death, the warmth withered out of the building like a ten-day-old bunch of end-of-summer flowers.

JW sat on Regina's bed, whispered to her, pulled a warmer under her chin, waited fifteen minutes, dimmed the night light, and tiptoed to his study. He beat his desk, tossed a folder, and scattered papers. The bottle of Scotch on the shelf stared him down. He rose and dropped back into the chair, for he never showed respect for characters on screen who used a bottle's contents to drown despair.

"Whiskey, you can look at me all you fuck like. There will be no action from over here."

Regina called those scenes the products of lazy writing, and he cringed at the memories of happier times.

Tragedies and misery combined were never so awful or unfortunate as to stop time. The Dawes' nights rolled into mornings, begotten days, birthed weeks, and stretched into unbearable months.

On a glorious South Florida morning four months into the accident and murders, Regina and JW sat over untouched breakfasts, haggard and sad. Their distant, tired eyes said they had traveled a million miles down separate lonely roads and hoped to meet at the fork if they got there.

Walloped by the tragedy, they remained solid, practical people who blamed mishap and grief as the catalyst. Not once did they blame each other or themselves for Mary's death, which was the norm amongst couples in tragedies. However, the despair in their souls never alleviated enough to allow them to return to their former social life. Regina ordered exotic hybrid roses and hibiscus plants. Consumed hours of each day nurturing them in her gardens as bits of rays rejuvenated the dark areas in her injured soul.

JW welcomed the birth of the color as it returned to Regina's cheeks. Still, he believed she equated her beautiful flowers with Mary. One morning, Regina gazed at the first double red hibiscus bloom for five minutes as if she didn't understand the miracle behind it and smiled. She drew closer to the plant, bent, and smiled with the flower. During those days, they rarely saw anyone outside of Regina's siblings.

JW dropped to his knees alongside her in the garden and spread black mulch over the red between the rose bushes. Their gloved hands touched. She squeezed his fingers and smiled at him. JW placed a dirty arm over her shoulder, giggled, and rested her head against his upper body. And they admired the new purplish blooms wet with morning dew.

The Dawes remained on their property otherwise for the funeral and JW's trip to the funeral home as they chose their path on the painful road back. They struck unavoidable bumps but relied on each other in the face of the angry storm.

Detective Councell called on JW once a week and paid respect to Regina whenever he encountered her in the front garden. After his last visit, JW and Regina agreed he only called when he smashed into the proverbial brick walls at the end of the dark road. JW listened to the police's lack of progress on the case with a wall-like blank face throughout the monologues. His teams of well-paid private investigators toiled, and none of them planned to prosecute anyone in court. His people, too, came up empty-handed, with no clues or rumors of one.

JW sat across from Regina, deep in reflection at the breakfast table on a Friday morning.

A super pro murdered his child, discarded the foul deed, and moved on as if they ran over fallen leaves. Accidents do happen and seem deliberate from the victims' point of view. But every nerve in his body pointed to murder.

What motives compelled a lunatic to launch a premeditated strike on his family? It must be to destroy him and his company.

JW shifted in his seat.

"Regina, our foundation is too strong for malice to hurt from the outside. Over the years, I made political donations to the left and ruffled feathers on the right. My people dug on the dark web and placed boots on unholy and holy grounds in their search for clues."

He held her hands across the table.

"If they find political footprints on my daughter's death, I shall eliminate them from the top down. Even those in large houses in DC would find no peace again in this world."

Regina smiled at JW.

"I mustered enough strength in the fourth month of our discomfort and planned to work back into my office schedule."

"I'm happy to hear, hon. It's time."

"I'll be going to work on Monday. Do you think you will be okay by yourself?" JW asked.

She squeezed his fingers.

"I'll be fine. I'm gonna bake also. Time has woken my fondness for sweets."

She envisioned Mary licking the batter off the stirring spoon, and she sniffled.

▲ ▲ ▲

On Monday morning, JW told his image in the mirror upstairs, I'm determined to emerge from the comfort of my anguish.

He took tentative steps down the stairs, his blue plaid suit sagging in areas it used to fill, but dapper enough for a dead man rising from the pit for the first time in four months.

At 8:00 a.m., he kissed Regina's cheek at the door, and she hugged him for a minute. JW sagged his shoulders to their lowest point and limped to the limo.

Regina eyed the closed door from the dining table and spooned fruit and warm cereal into her mouth. Her mom only ate cold grains, something she still could not wrap her palate around after so many years.

Mary's birth was difficult. Doctor Reed informed her and JW that she would never conceive again. The news devastated her, but JW's love and strength got her through those difficult months. Over the years, they poured every ounce of love on Mary.

Regina grew up to be the baby of two girls from pediatrician parents, and they lived in a comfortable house two blocks from the one percenter in The Gables. Regina and her sisters ran alongside the more affluent children at their parents' office on Valencia Avenue from age six. At a birthday party of a childhood friend, she met JW months before her eighteenth birthday. They became inseparable from the night they met, and their marriage stretched into one extended honeymoon.

She feared the future without Mary.

Wait, she caught herself acknowledging Mary's demise for the first time. Regina placed the bowl to her head, slurped the last mouthful of her cereal, picked up her dishes, headed to the sink, and returned carrying a dustpan.

"Oh, Lord, where do I start?"

She shook her head. The doorbell rang, and her sister Madeline let herself inside. Madeline saw the broom in Regina's hand, grinned, raced, and embraced Regina.

"My sister is back, baby. My sister Regina is back."

▲ ▲ ▲

Surprised employees greeted JW, and he waved a feeble hand as he ducked into his office. Van Drake followed him, and JW eyed a thin folder on his desk with Van Drake's neat handwriting on the cover. JW gazed across at him.

"We found nothing, not a squawk or a whisper popped on the byways or from the Dark Web," Van Drake said.

JW rifled through the document, and his eyes strayed to the phone.

"I'm asking you again. Do you believe in random?" JW asked.

"Random can never be this good."

JW glanced back at his desk.

"Let's talk later. I've got calls to make."

"Okay, boss."

Van exited the office, pleased that he could speak to his boss on equal terms. Nevertheless, he felt that he had failed Mary, and most nights sleep eluded him. He and his men concluded ghosts couldn't drive hit-and-run vehicles, and those facts remained the only ones gleaned from his investigations.

"A sly killer laughed and continued to fuck his way through life like angels on milk and honey through the halls of Heaven," Van mumbled.

The door lock clicked, and JW dialed a disposable phone.

The call caught Illisya in the kitchen preparing an early breakfast.

"Babes, you've made my day," Illisya quipped.

"It's over two months since we spoke. I'm not sure if you remembered me," JW said.

"I'll not travel a yard if you're not at my side," Illisya said.

"Regina went down and is not back up in shape yet, and today is my first day at work."

"You are at work? That's wonderful news, babes," Illisya assured.

She turned off the stove and raced into her bedroom with Bluetooth in her ears.

"These few minutes brought me immense pleasure and some semblance of joy, Illisya."

JW cried into the receiver, consumed by the inner guilt his confession had fostered. Illisya hauled on a UPS uniform and placed baggy sweats over it.

"Sorry, Illisya. I'll call you again in the morning."

"Okay, babes. I'm looking forward to hearing your voice."

He hung up and held the phone against his pants leg.

"Is it possible to love Regina and feel compelled to touch Illisya's essence as my own?"

The symbolic implications of Regina's red rose with the morning dew carved his soul and drew him into a contemplative vacuum. He visited it for days until it faded into a drooping blob.

The dynamics of life, place, and things played out on the universal plain, mindless of mortals' trivial or major concerns.

He experienced a philosophical and poetic moment, gripped the phone, and a warmness radiated through his body.

In the months that JW didn't call, he deposited her allowances into her account, paid her lease from a secret fund she suspected, and her project ran on schedule from her end.

The conversation elated her and set the mood for the rest of her day.

The police should have called on her already, because they played an essential role in her machinery. Anyway, she followed her plotline and exercised her patience. Every passing day distanced her taillights from the chasing pack, and she never glanced behind her.

"The forever waiting dragged on my nerves at times. How hadn't the damn police come across my name yet? Unbelievable, and JW went back to work."

She wanted to see their case file, and only her iron willpower kept her from hacking Detective Councell's computer.

"One cannot be too careful when one disturbed a hornet's nest. One of the critters could jump your barricade and sting you from the blindside, and there is more work to do."

Illisya gazed up at the ceiling.

"My palace gleamed and got closer. Any day now, the door will swing open, and I shall sit on my throne."

She bolted through the front door. Thirty minutes later, she rode a motorcycle up a UPS truck ramp parked before a seedy warehouse bay in the industrial area of Hialeah. A large person leaned inside the recess of the warehouse wall like a tilted mannequin as she pushed the ramp up in the vehicle, ran around, and drove away.

Illisya boarded the Fisher Island Ferry, disembarked, and rode up Fisher Island Drive, placed a package on a pistol with a silencer on the seat. She slowed, approaching JW's mansion. Regina and Madeline gardened on a rose bed in the front of the house. The vehicle slowed and continued.

"I might as well kill some time over at Gulfstream Racetrack later, after I attend a photo shoot."

Her new friend, the jockey from Venezuela's girlfriend, might sit on a winner or two. Yes, Maria always has winning tips for her.

Up to the infamous day of musing, she didn't understand how a woman over six feet tall dated a four-foot rider.

Her Mr. Haynes knew the rider when he mastered Calder Racetrack. After he moved his tack up north, her Dad relayed to Mr. Falkner what a down-on-his-luck jock named Gray told him. He lamented that if the boss were still there, he would order the jockey room to send him on to cover his lawyer's expenses. Gray did nine months in prison soon after for repeated DUIs.

Illisya ditched the truck in a parking lot on SW 32nd Avenue and hailed a cab. At 1:55 a.m., she strolled to her car with a professional photographer's camera around her neck, checked the time on her phone, and cranked her radio to a local music station. She drove to NE Miami, drumming on her wheel to heavy bass, in a jovial mood. She rolled into the Breakfast Box parking lot on Dixie Highway as a waitress sat Kali and Dread at an outdoor table. Illisya took a dozen photos of Dread from her car in the parking lot.

"Kali, you're out of the loop. I wanted to do the horses, not drag down the slot's alleys."

The exhilarating sensation she experienced as her horse ran by the field to the post she could not reproduce anywhere on the planet. It was like Pluto and the Earth when compared to the dull feeling she experienced during a business kill.

Hours later, Illisya left the apartment armed with five hundred dollars to bet and lunch.

She reached Gulfstream fifteen minutes before the first post and searched in vain for her Venezuelan acquaintance at her habitual location. But she ran into her bald-headed Jamaican acquaintance, Father Amin, the Maiden Specialist, and he gave her a twenty-five to one two-year-old maiden to play.

"Bank it in the Pick 4 and go all and all in the remaining three races. Or you can buy it to win," Father Amin said.

"How are you playing it?" Illisya asked.

"I love the thrill of the exotics. A mere win ticket is dull on the excitement scale for me."

"Okay, I wanna roll with you, but how did you find a horse that hasn't run yet?" Illisya asked.

"Bloodline handicapping. It's a four-and-a-half-furlong race, and his sire drops first time winners for a joke. All the other million-dollar horses in the field are bred for the Derby. The top jocks rode them, and they took the bulk of the bets, but the distance is too short for them."

"I got you. I don't doubt you, but I want to understand the method of the madness," Illisya said.

"Oh, yeah, a horse that cost ten K is gonna run the half million and over nags off their feet. Madness indeed," Father Amin said.

"So, where's the Rat Poison Dread?" Illisya asked.

"He migrated to NYC. They have a fine collection of rat poisons up there."

"I loved his mantra. If this one loses, I'm talking rat poison," Illisya said.

Father Amin laughed and bumped Illisya's fist.

Illisya fed money into a betting kiosk.

"I want to still laugh carefree like my man Father Amin when I reach his age. I wager he's not into religion."

She bought the ticket for three hundred and fifty dollars, purchased an ice cream cone, made her way to the trackside, and waited for the thunder of hooves to pound her heart. The anchor of her bet led from the gate and won by three widened lengths at thirty to one. She retreated from the sun to an umbrella table and waited for the three other legs to run. Illisya ordered a club soda and kicked back as she conjured pictures of JW and her in the winner's enclosure at the Kentucky Derby.

"My first classic horse, I shall name The Young Tycoon."

After the last leg, she signed her ticket and searched for Father Amin.

"Doc, where's your friend?"

"He collected a piss pot load and went to Aventura Mall before he flew to Jamaica."

Illisya chuckled.

"I know he took care of you guys, but here's two thousand dollars to split between you, Milo, Mikey, and Indian."

Those cohorts sat together for years and shared their winnings, something hardly anyone else does, except the island guys. Her Pop couldn't explain it to her as a child, and the Maiden Specialist led the pack. Her pocketbook bulged with six thousand and change dollars on her way home.

"Meg gal, your medication and grocery tan up."

She giggled in her car.

Chapter 22

On the second morning back at work, JW entered his office minutes after 8:00 a.m. and broke out a new burner phone before settling into serious business. Illisya's cell rang. The device sat atop her winnings from the day before on the coffee table. She raced from the kitchen, snatched it on the third ring, and plopped onto the sofa.

"Hello, hon."

They spoke for thirty minutes, and Ellysia's expressions shifted between happiness, excitement, and a primitive seriousness as she wedged her say into the conversation.

JW ended with a promise.

"I'll call you the same time every weekday morning."

"I loved that, JW. You're my light."

After the call, JW smirked at his desk. The night before, Regina opened the front door and greeted him. The act warmed his soul, and her body pulsed against his.

"I'm waiting for her to mention adoption, and I'm sure she will soon."

JW kept his promise and called Illisya five mornings a week but did not visit her apartment or see her elsewhere. Over the past month, he chaired three departmental meetings, consulted with department heads, reassured overseas portfolio holders, and dragged himself back into the stream's flow. On a Thursday, he summoned Milla Williams for a progress report on the multimillion-dollar portfolio she inherited from Bill. As minutes bled into hours, JW slipped into his habitual self, his body blooming like Regina's flower wet with morning dew.

Three months after JW's first workday call, Illisya dribbled a ball on a soccer field beneath a dark, swollen sky. Lightning ripped the air, and the remaining parents and kids fled to their cars. The delay by the law gnawed at her patience. She kicked the ball into the net, frustrated.

"They should've nailed me as a suspect already. Their ineptitude bogged down my operation and slowed my schedule to a crawl."

Dread rolled into the park as other cars exited. He sprang from the vehicle and opened Kali's door. His slim-built body could have slipped into Illisya's five ten frame without excess if they merged. His trademark stringy dreadlocks hung in his face like a shredded curtain as he leaned against the door. Kali hugged him, pecked his lips, and walked toward Illisya.

"What's up, Illisya?" Dread called.

"We're hanging out."

Dread glanced at the rain-heavy sky and shook his locks.

"I didn't know you had something to show."

"If you knew, you wouldn't be alive today," Kali said.

Dread grinned.

"Come chat with us. Illisya's moving to the mountains soon."

"A mountain without weed. No thanks. See you later."

"How's the late game tonight?" Illisya asked.

"Oh yeah. De Heat ago jerk a pot of Curry from San Francisco tonight."

"Get on with it. Don't hide in your shadows like me."

"You know what? I, man, gonna smoke a big head spliff and hold a meds on what you said."

Dread grinned and drove off. Kali and Illisya sat side by side at midfield.

Before Kali lured Dread away from his ganja plantation and coordinator job at the famous hotel on Negril Beach, she told Illisya how he nailed her sensual sites the first time on the beach. He repeated the feat in his weed field and carried it into her bed.

Kali gazed up at the pregnant sky.

"I'm not moving," Illisya said.

"It's unnatural for girls to fraternize in bushes with creepers for too long."

"You know my Dad, Bill, and I camped for years."

"God designed girls for indoor plumbing and warm water. God, I miss Bill."

"I miss him more. I was devastated. I couldn't even attend his funeral."

They dribbled toward the goal as thunder rolled and the sky opened, as if summoned to cleanse two wayward souls.

"Bill and I planned lunch for Wednesday. He died Tuesday night," Kali said.

"It hurts. Want a secret? Guess who blew Bill before he died."

Kali froze, eyes bulging, mouth agape.

"Unbelievable. He was like your brother."

"I treated it as a training exercise."

"What do you mean?"

"I didn't want to appear amateur to someone you haven't met."

"Bill said he introduced you to some hotshot."

"He did?"

"I planned to needle the name out of him at lunch."

"Hearing it from you helps."

"How?"

"Knowing his last plans, even small ones, warms my sense of him."

"I don't understand you."

Grape-sized rain slammed the field.

Illisya sprawled onto her back in the saturated grass. Kali followed as Florida lightning chopped the sky and reflected in their shades. A bolt slammed beyond the goalpost. Thunder cracked. Neither flinched.

"Everything unfolds like state secrets with you."

"When did life become a rush?" Illisya asked.

"A rush? You've been running with a man nearly a year."

"I'll guarantee you a bridesmaid ticket when we return from the sticks."

"Wonderful. Can I meet the fucking groom before the wedding?"

Illisya gaped.

"He is a groom, right?"

"He's been traumatized."

"Well, call me a virgin."

"He'll be back soon. Regardless, we're locked into a journey through the perpetual cosmos."

Kali rolled her eyes.

"Are you the piece of music that refused the dancer's steps?"

"Get married and exclude me and find out."

They laughed and embraced like lovers on the grass.

"So, you killed your mother?"

"Fuck no. Heart attack."

"How'd you induce it?"

"Dread and I crashed her racist lady's fundraiser. A White House Evangelical Guy who kissed the president's ass twice daily turned green and dove through a French window."

"And?"

"We jumped on the banquet table and dove into doggy style. I screamed louder than the day I scared birds on Dread's mountain."

"Shocking."

"Old racist hags dropped like gassed extras in horror movies."

Illisya snickered and slapped the soggy ground.

"Adrinia MacArthur apologized yesterday. Said she wasn't strong enough to do what I did."

"Isn't she enslaved to her mother's program?"

"She's a pretender waiting for the inheritance. She plans to marry a Black man the moment her mother dies and hopes it wipes out the rest."

"Tell them time isn't part of the promise."

"I'm growing. I see pure human spirits now."

"Many are monsters in disguise," Illisya said.

"Our lives are beacons in stormy days, don't you think?"

They made obscene sounds as Illisya attempted a backstroke in one foot of water.

"I'm swimming before I leave."

Lightning reflected in their lenses, twisting Kali's calm face into terror. Her body twitched, reliving something buried.

Debris floated around their waists in the water. Kali's body stiffened, like she fell in a trance. Illisya shook her. She jolted and forced a crooked smile.

"I drifted for a moment."

"Into the nuisance, didn't you?"

"I slip sometimes."

"I told you to kick it."

"You're steel. I'm all pussy."

Kali searched for Illisya's eyes.

"Could you do it again like that night?"

"Why?"

"You made it look easy. Experts say the first kill makes the second easier."

Kali looked away, regretting the question.

"You wanted him dead?" Illisya asked.

"Yes, but."

"Not all chores are personal. Dangerous ones belong in business columns. Outsourcing strangers was reckless."

"I worry about you. Experts are rarely wrong," Kali said.

"Toss it. Ditch it."

Kali bowed her head.

"Life dies inside apology bubbles."

"You're right."

They embraced, eyes speaking behind lenses. Kali believed Jack was Illisya's first victim and not her father.

"How were you and your Pops?"

"Father and daughter. Not wilderness bonding like you."

"The world is wilderness."

"I thought it was a ghetto."

They floated on their backs.

Illisya imagined herself as wind, rain, lightning, thunder, and a born hunter-gatherer. She wielded free will and cut through jungles without fear. Otherwise, she'd be a politician outdoing fools in Congress.

She smiled behind her glasses. Kali lifted on one elbow and stared at her friend's iron-hard façade.

Chapter 23

A must-attend business meeting arose in Washington, DC, and JW agonized on his drive home about leaving Regina alone.

JW and Regina sat by the pool two evenings before the trip, sipping fruit smoothies.

"Did you sprinkle alcohol inside these?" JW asked.

"I made them from my Jamaican Cocktails Recipe Book. Everything calls for rum and weed."

"Ganja?" JW asked.

"Miss Sativa thrived in my back garden, clothed in her golden buds," Regina said.

Her eyes flamed at him.

"It took me back to the elephant on the lawn. Still, I'm reluctant to leave you here alone. I think I should take you with me."

"You go nip at those pesky barracudas and show them you're still a shark. I'm not in traveling shape yet."

Regina placed her hand over his on the wing of the beach chair.

"Go bite them, hammerhead."

"Are you sure I'm not a great white?"

She slapped his shoulder and ended the discussion. Van Drake would accompany him to the capital.

▲ ▲ ▲

The morning before the trip, JW called Illisya.

"I'm flying to DC tonight for a 10:00 a.m. meeting tomorrow."

"When will you be back, hon?"

"I should be home by 4:00 p.m. tomorrow at the latest."

"Commercial?" Illisya asked.

"Oh no. I'm flying my private jet. No sense owning a multimillion-dollar aircraft and walking a thousand miles."

Illisya whickered into his ear.

"Safe journey, love. I'll be here when you return."

They spoke for a few more minutes and hung up.

Illisya exhaled, relieved.

"My cue. For a beat, I thought he'd invite me."

On the eve of the meeting, Illisya rode her bike in a bulky black leather jacket and helmet, trailing JW's limo through murderous Miami traffic to Miami Executive Airport.

She cruised past the gate as Van Drake, whom she believed capable only of digging up school records, removed luggage from the vehicle.

She relished the hunter-gatherer life amid poisonous serpents that posed no real danger.

"Later in life, I should teach my methods to young people who want more than gold digging. On the dark web, of course. A bad gal schoolyard. A deep, wonderful place. Like dinosaur land, where hunters become prey in a blink."

She waited until the jet roared into the evening sky, turned around, rode east on 36th Street and pulled into Meg's driveway at dusk. She tucked the bike behind the house, slipped inside, returned with a red tote, and hurried off. As she rounded the bend, she cast her habitual glance at Ron's bedroom window.

"I swear Marine Ron watches my every move. If I told folks to fight their war and build wealth, they'd call me unpatriotic. Look now, you got sick and they got rich, as Meg says. I need her back on her feet."

She glanced once more into the darkness and disappeared.

Ron watched through the blinds, waited five minutes, and crept outside. He mounted Illisya's motorcycle and mimicked a high-speed chase, waving his gun like a cowboy. He leaned, tilted, straightened, and raised his arm in triumph.

▲ ▲ ▲

JW called Regina from his private jet.

"Are you are doing okay, baby?"

"I'm fine. You worry too much."

Despite her assurance, a knot formed in his stomach for reasons he couldn't name. They spoke until 8:00 p.m.

▲ ▲ ▲

Mr. Dofus sat on a bench at Kendall Mall, slurping ice cream. Thirty yards away, Figama's neon sign glowed seductively. He dialed a cheap burner, his bloated gut begging him to discard the sundae and his rain-soaked suit.

"Hello."

"May I speak to Mr. Dawes?" Mr. Dofus asked.

"Who is this?"

"Are you Mrs. Dawes?"

His voice climbed into a whiny, artificial pitch.

"Ma'am, the police have botched your daughter's investigation."

Pain tugged at Regina's voice.

"I'm calling my husband."

"I don't have much time. I know something about your daughter's death."

"What do you know?"

"Did he follow me in here? Oh Jesus, I have got to go."

"No. Please," Regina begged.

"I don't trust phones."

"Where are you?"

"Kendall Mall. Figama. I'm leaving town."

He shifted on the bench.

"How will I recognize you?"

"I know you. I worked for your husband."

"My husband isn't home."

"I'm sorry. I'm in danger. I must go."

Children with Mickey and Minnie balloons laughed nearby. A balloon slipped free. Mr. Dofus chased it and returned the rodent caricature.

A thousand thoughts assaulted Regina. If she didn't go, she might lose the truth forever.

"I'll meet you," she said.

"Come alone."

"I will."

"The third floor is clear for parking. I parked there a minute ago. Hurry, ma'am."

Mr. Dofus dropped the phone into a trash bin.

▲ ▲ ▲

At 8:59 p.m., Regina parked on the third floor. Mr. Dofus sprang from behind a vehicle and shot her twice in the head. JW's jet touched down in DC at the exact moment.

The killer slid the gun away, stuffed his hands in his pockets, and walked off.

▲ ▲ ▲

Fifty-six minutes later, Mr. Dofus cruised on a dim corner of NW 12 Avenue in Liberty City and pulled onto an abandoned building's driveway. He removed a piece of luggage from the passenger seat, scampered away, and left the windows down with the key in the ignition.

Mr. Dofus waddled onto a crowded city bus on NW12 Avenue. She eyed the empty seat beside the Sad Bum and stood for a block. However, an itch-like feeling in her head compelled her to sit. A Young Couple kissed and giggled in front of Sad Bum and Mr. Dofus as if they cavorted in their bedroom.

The passengers used handheld electronic devices except for Sad Bum and a parched, lips-distressed woman across the aisle.

The woman squeezed her right finger on her lap like she planned to break off all five. While she stared at her demise at a crossroads, like a harbinger coming at her.

Mr. Dofus adjusted his body from the man's rags. Still, the Bum pivoted his head, and his ocean-deep eyes locked on Dofus' sour disposition.

"Sir, did you do unto others as you would love them to do unto you today?"

"It's none of your damn business what I did or didn't do," Mr. Dofus said.

"Simply put, everything is my business, and free will is an expensive commodity," Sad Bum said.

Mr. Dofus gaped into the man's eyes, and they reminded him of a star-filled sky from the darkness of a forest. He swore the eyes reflected a dark blue haze a second before. Mr. Dofus's body tingled, and he frowned at the strange sensation as it ran through his body.

"I speak of virtue. The mundane. The arcane," sad bum said.

"Do I know you?"

"No."

"Let's keep it that way."

"You've saddened me."

Mr. Dofus grinned, and the man's dirty face glowed momentarily. Mr. Dofus' smirk faded, and his eyes dipped like a cowered dog's tail.

▲ ▲ ▲

Ron mimicked a speed biker for hours astride Illisya's motorcycle into the dark, listened to insects' antics, and faked a speed biker for ten minutes every half an hour. He dismounted, weary, and walked backward across up to his front door. Three minutes ticked by. Ron darted back outside shirtless without his gun, held his head, rocked, and collapsed in the driveway as his Mother's car pulled up. She dialed emergency services, ran to him, and lifted his head in her lap.

"Ron did you take your medication."

"I was riding back and forth through the world, Mom."

"Of course, baby. You'll be fine now, Mom is here, son."

She closed her eyes, held her head back, and rocked his head in her lap.

▲ ▲ ▲

The bus stopped near the VA Hospital on NW 16th Street. Sad Bum stood, brushed against the Distressed Woman, and her face lit up at his touch.

"Everything's going to be fine. You're going to get well soon, my baby. Yes, I'm certain of it now, baby," the distressed woman said to herself.

Sad Bum stumbled off the bus. Mr. Dofus rushed to the door on a second thought. He shuffled ten paces ahead of Mr. Dofus at a relaxed pace on the warm night with the sidewalk emptied of pedestrians.

A horn honked, and Mr. Dofus whipped his head behind and back to an empty sidewalk. His eyes roved in every direction, and he climbed to a higher elevation through an opening in the hedges. He combed the night, but the Sad Bum disappeared. Mr. Dofus hastened up a concrete walkway to the VA hospital emergency entrance. Two ambulances unloaded patients, the first responders rolled away two accident victims, and EMS pushed Ron from the second ambulance, secured in a straitjacket. Ron flicked his head side to side, and cold sweat flew like from a sprinkler. Two Nurses hovered over him at the lift, and Mrs. Gibson mopped his forehead.

"I said, Ron, did you take your medication? And he kept saying yes, Mom, yes."

"Chill, Mom. One day in the city is a day in the universe," Ron said.

"Yeah, right?" Mrs. Gibson said.

The nurses wheeled Ron into the elevator.

▲ ▲ ▲

The VA Hospital's furnace roared like a caged monster in the deep, hot basement. Counting the grime and trash on the floor, the people who swabbed upstairs never took their mops and buckets down there.

Mr. Dofus skipped down the stairs as if he worked in the boiler room, stood inches from the incinerator, and peeled his hair off. A bundle fell free, and he tossed a wig and mask into the fire. Yanked his potbelly free, revealed Illisya under disguise. She removed pieces of synthetics from her face and stepped out of her crumpled black pants. Illisya dusted lint off her designer jeans, took off her coat, and exposed her red tank top. She removed the red tote from the shopping bag, folded the paper, and tossed everything in the fire.

▲ ▲ ▲

Meg lay lifeless in her hospital bed on the fourth floor. A distressed Illisya hurried in, kissed Meg on her cheek, and the old girl opened her eyes as Illisya placed the red duffle beside the bed.

Tears streaked down Illisya's cheeks, and Meg shook her head. Illisya brought her ear down to Meg's mouth, kissed her forehead, and nodded as Meg whispered.

Meg closed her eyes; an emotionless Illisya placed a chair at the bedside, turned on the TV, and Mrs. Dawes' murder played on the late news.

"Two down and one to go. Time visited and gave me the handle of the blade," Illisya said.

Meg's eyes opened, and Illisya held her feeble hand.

Chapter 24

A flustered Detective Councell addressed his task force in a conference room at MPD HQ. Anxious, edgy failure lines drew around his mouth and dulled his eyes into a matte glaze.

The Dawes woman's death could bring the FBI down on his back, and he had a personal stake on the table. He told Peggy Sue that he would resign if the Feds took his case. Failing to the suited motherfuckers from DC, he likened it to when someone forced raw gall down a parched throat. The idea of the overfed dogs butting in hurt more than the demise of Hurtz.

Councell glanced at his stern, eager colleagues as they waited for their orders and pounded a fist into his palm.

"We've done too much work to toss our files on the G-guys' lap. I wanted the perp in a cell yesterday."

"We've got a person of interest caught on camera in the mall's parking lot, about the time of the killing," Blundell said.

Blundell handed out Mr. Dofus's photos, and Officer Willis beamed.

"Hold a minute. We've got this photo on file."

Willis displayed Mr. Dofus's photo on his tablet.

"An ATM camera took these the night Detective Hurtz died," Willis said.

"We canvassed the neighborhood and every hotel within a five-mile radius at the time, but no one remembered the subject."

"However, he showed up again at the promenade at another murder?" Councell asked.

Constable Davis handed Councell a file.

"It came in a few minutes ago, sir."

"Who's Illisya Haynes?" Councell asked.

"Ron Gibson romanced her car two days ago. We ran the plate, dug into her finances, found her jobless, and owning a hundred-thousand-dollar sports car."

"Interesting."

"She also attended Central High alongside Bill and Lacey Kelly."

"Where's she now?" Councell asked.

"Surveillance is on her, sir."

"Get to work on her and put the last time she wet her bed in black and white on my desk yesterday," Councell said.

The cops dispersed, and Councell plopped at his desk.

"Could the assassin be a woman? No wonder we profiled a male for an apple tree in an orange grove. But where does the beer-gut man fit into the scheme of things?" Councell asked.

▲ ▲ ▲

Early the following day, on a bright, sunny South Florida morning, Illisya pulled into a dealership lot on NW 7th Avenue. The city could be heaven if the summer showers fell between 3:00 a.m. and 5:00 a.m., rather than noon to 4:00 p.m.

Illisya turned east, swallowed a mouthful of warm morning air, and smiled at the sky. Rumors said the president ordered the governor to end the fake rain that kept interrupting golf in Florida.

"Bye-bye, spoilers of days," Illisya grinned.

Kali parked and paced the sidewalk on her phone in front of the dealership. Illisya figured she ordered Viagra from one of those not-so-upfront Cuban pharmacies for Dread, and they were late on the delivery.

I bet she drove the poor boy onto something he doesn't need, and they're gonna find him before his thirtieth birthday, out of touch with reality, either with Kali on top or beneath him. He should've stayed on Negril Beach and at his ganja farm, cooked Ital food, and smoked weed if he'd known what she knew.

Illisya ducked into the dealership office and rejoined Kali minutes later. They drove south on Seventh Avenue.

"I can't make breakfast. Drop me off at Tesso," Illisya said.

"Do you want me to come and get you?" Kali asked.

"No, I'll walk back."

"Okay, see you," Kali said.

Tesso, a high-rise office building, stood four blocks away and shared a clear view of the dealership from the upper floor. Illisya lingered at the entrance, and her tail pulled up across from the building. She swung her head in a wide arc, painted them, and barged through the door.

Illisya opened a fire door on the fourth floor and climbed the stairs to the roof; she and her old man broke into one of the offices once there on a mission for the late Mr. Falkner nine years ago.

While the stakeout team kept tabs, a tech team flashed badges, descended on the service department, and waved a warrant around. Law enforcement techs in overalls erected barricades and screened Illisya's car from peering eyes. They pretended to search the vehicle but hid listening devices. Illisya observed the operation through binoculars from the high-rise four blocks away and nodded her approval.

"We should've been long past this stage already. I've laid crumbs for you to follow to the coup de grâce," Illisya said.

A technical team disguised as servicemen wiretapped Illisya's apartment. Illisya guffawed as the operation unfolded on her tablet on the rooftop, and her eyes flashed with a sharp, battle-ax edge glint. A nasty tech searched her underwear drawer, inspected each item, and replaced them.

She wondered several times what drove the fascination men carried for women's underwear. They took their fetish to the stores, and dead-eyed fellows came to life at the underwear display.

"But hey, we all needed something to help us pull through the dull days."

Illisya spent an hour in the building. The police detail switched cars and moved to the far left. She spotted them as they fought not to gawk at her exposed legs in her short mini. Illisya smiled, and it exploded into a beautiful thing as she held her head high, peered at the cops, chattered on her cell, and strutted along.

A mechanic rolled her car out onto the sidewalk, the oil changed, and the body cleaned and shined. Illisya tipped the man a twenty-dollar bill, and his guilty eyes gave him away as he contemplated telling her about the search.

Illisya stopped at the supermarket on her ride home and later barged through her door, in an angelic mood, with two heavy brown paper grocery bags. She placed the bags on the kitchen counter and opened her blinds. The late evening sunrays danced through the blades, and she gazed into the sun with spite. She stripped her clothes one piece at a time like a pro, drank a glass of juice, keyed her phone to the music box, and danced dirty on the couch, chairs, and table to a random mixture of reggae, rock, blues, and country. The station house would burn to ash if they installed cameras instead of audio devices.

▲ ▲ ▲

A tag team of detectives tailed JW's limo while two other teams bugged his home and office. JW dragged himself through each moment of the elongated, woeful days, hunched under his sorrows and hurt.

On a bright Sunday morning, he turned off the AC in the mansion and plopped on the deep burgundy leather sofa in his study. If the cops wanted to bug the spot he sat on, they would have to lift and replace his dilapidated butt afterward. He buried his head in his hands for long, agonizing minutes.

Someone was out to destroy him. He took a short business trip to Washington, DC, and returned to his wife's dead body. Who could be so cruel and cunning? Could it be the Russian oligarch? He held federally sanctioned frozen assets belonging to them. What about the Chinese interests? He didn't manage a portfolio for either regime but invested money for their nationals and expatriates, sometimes under the scrutiny of tax authorities. It could also be Mossad, because his company invested money and enriched their martial enemies. They may be the ones who taught him a lesson. The professional disposal of his family felt to him like state-agency involvement.

JW laid the groundwork for his revenge and waited for the perpetrators to unleash hell upon themselves. He arranged to acquire world-destroying revenge on the black market if he found any governments or their agencies culpable in his family's death.

He leaned back into the soft leather and dried his tears, for cocked guns didn't cry. They took aim and waited.

Another Miami Monday morning dazzled in all its glory in downtown Miami. Councell exited his service vehicle in the county lot at 50 NW 2nd Avenue and dashed toward the courthouse. Illisya, disguised as a meter maid, picked his auto's lock and installed CIA-issued spyware under the seats and in the consoles.

She went over to a table at the Miami-Dade Metro Station at Government Center and broke out a tablet. She relayed the bugs to a state server in Tampa and back to her device.

So far, the law rode on her tail. However, in the coming months, instead of finding her guilty, the men in blue would prove her innocence without a doubt to the court and JW.

"While I cried like a broken addict in distress."

She closed her tablet.

"My unlawful gigs elevated themselves above forensic TV crap. Time and events shall prove me right."

Illisya concluded a gratifying morning at the office, developed an appetite for a Jamaican feast, and headed north. She hadn't been to her parents' home for a while, but Stamma, the landscaper, kept the old place immaculate. Meg came out of the hospital two and a half weeks ago; she should surprise the old girl. She exited I-95 at the NW 183rd Street exit, stopped at BB West Indian Food at the Seventh Avenue corner, bought the needed ingredients, and proceeded to her parents' empty house.

"God bless Meg and her culinary skills."

She swung into the ackee tree, handpicked dozens of fruits, and dropped them in a pile on the ground. Half an hour later, she pulled up at Meg's house.

She planned to surprise the old girl with ackee and veggie delight, her favorite dish, and clean the house to invigorate her mind.

Meg met her on the old porch, took the ackee from her, and hobbled into the kitchen without a word between them until they hit the black counter.

"If you're giving Ron a plate, you'll have to bring it to him. I don't want him over here," Illisya said.

"Are you getting to be like your fucking father?" Meg asked.

"Yes, I am, for you should be cleaning the ackees without being told."

They laughed and hugged each other in an exhibition of pure love.

"Those are your bell peppers, your cauliflower, carrots, your string beans, your salted cod, onion, and garlic. Where is your Jamaican yellow yam, flour, and green bananas?"

"This is strictly a veggie delight."

"These Jamaican people brought their ackee trees and menus over here," Meg said.

"Fuck de Jamaicans."

"I've Jamaican relatives, and when I die, I'm gonna haunt your ass when you're having sex. I'm gonna spread my wings across the ceiling over your head and make angry ghostly faces."

"Who said I look into the fucking ceiling during sex?"

Meg flung an ackee seed and nailed her in the gut.

▲ ▲ ▲

A combined force of Miami Gardens, Miami-Dade, and Miami City lawmen invaded Illisya's childhood home thirty minutes after she vacated the property. They picked the front door lock, searched the empty house, filed through the back to the steel shed door, and gathered before it, shocked.

The sign posted on the door read: Officers, I'm open.

Their enthusiasm drained, and they swung the massive door open to the shed: empty, bone-white painted walls.

"What do you think she stored in here?" Blundell asked a Miami Gardens uniformed sergeant.

"Enough evidence to put away Congress and the president for years."

"The walls of Heaven are not this clean."

As the men and women drifted off the property, Councell wondered if Illisya was a demon or a woman.

Chapter 25

Seven months after Regina's death, a cheery Illisya entertained a haggard and gloomy JW in their regular clothes across her bed.

"My situation worsens daily since Regina's death," JW said.

He leaped to his feet and tramped around the room, his thoughts incoherent and his mind a shell of his former self.

Illisya propped herself on an elbow; her eyes shone like a fisherman who hauled the ultimate catch from troubled waters and landed it on his deck. JW took a vial of Viagra from the night table and read the label.

"Pace yourself, hon. Seven months are not bad for what you endured."

She reached for JW's hand, and he sat back on the bed, dejected.

"I killed my wife and daughter as if I did it with my own hands."

"No, JW, you shouldn't blame yourself."

"My Dad dragged me into fools' paradise. I went without protest, got comfortable in forbidden beds, and strode a perverted blind path. It's my fault, Illisya, and Karma sent her big bad friend, retribution, to fuck me."

"What did your father do, babes? Why would Karma shaft an angel like you?"

She caressed JW's back, her fingers tapping along his spine.

"Where does this Karma guy live, JW?"

JW rolled his eyes at her and fought back a smile.

He said he wouldn't, but he broke down and cried anyway, his body jerking hard enough to feel like something inside might break. Illisya massaged his shoulders but let him drain his grief. JW cried at his guilt and pain and found no comfortable place outside Illisya's presence, and it scared him as much as he embraced it.

"The elusive perp ran free as if he didn't commit a crime, and the pain of not swatting someone grew harder daily. But if I ever get another chance at life, it will be different," JW said.

"Your problems are not physical, and I'm not going anywhere, babes. I'm here forever either way," Illisya said.

"If I didn't have you, I would've caved during the deep dark months since. I would've lost myself in a forbidden abyss."

Illisya embraced him.

"I'm a changed man, Illisya. Please, God, grant me another chance," JW prayed.

Illisya kissed his wet cheeks.

Councell sipped coffee from a Styrofoam cup beside Blundell in a surveillance van outside Illisya's apartment. A sheen grew on Councell's skin, and he glowed as if he oiled down on South Beach among elite sunbathers daily. He caught his reflection in the rearview mirror and winked.

He walked on air from the day his wife returned to his bed and brought all the honey from Heaven, minus the bees.

Blundell studied the building through binoculars.

"She's fucking good," Councell said.

"I used to think we were better, but I'm not so sure anymore."

"Blundell, how come we never catch criminals from the intent stage?"

Blundell gave his partner a curious look.

"How many partners have you eaten through, over the years?"

JW's voice echoed through the system.

"These fucking pills are not for me."

"Fucking pills, they're too," Illisya giggled.

Something smashed into the wall, and Blundell jumped from his distant thoughts.

"I'm in a box here. I need to breathe. Oh shit. Did I commit myself to green hell?" JW asked.

"Yes, darling. As I told you, a trek through virgin forest for a week will sharpen your blade."

"I can't believe I dug my own damn grave," JW said.

"The green will do what concrete couldn't do and rejuvenate your soul, mind, and body. Wouldn't you want to experience the thrill of life again?" Illisya asked.

"Mmm, rub here, please."

"You're tight like a scared virgin, dear," Illisya said.

"As the analogy goes, am I a witness to the final metaphor?"

"We brave cosmic winds every day and fight the odds to be masters of our lives," Illisya said.

"Profound and compelling."

"Thanks. Do you play soccer?" Illisya asked.

"I did, back in college."

"I find soccer most stimulating," Illisya said.

"Where would I get the energy?"

"They're dormant, waiting to erupt."

"So, tell me, who dumped the Arctic on me?" JW asked.

"You're Noah's boat, situated in a perpetual slot of place and time."

"I'll be the critical spectator for you, if you'll stick to popular sound bites," JW said.

"You're bigly and tremendously nice, sir."

"Wasn't he the one who stomped the brakes when not the brake person on the runaway train?" JW asked.

Illisya laughed, and Councell cringed as it dawned on him that she was playing with the bugs. He would wager his last dollar that she knew about the plant from the first day and fed his officers hours of incoherent babble.

"Your shrink has got to be in therapy," JW said.

More laughter assailed the men, and they searched each other desperately for answers.

"How could one girl slaughter four people, including a cop, and we can't find a shred of evidence to arrest her?" Blundell asked.

"A smudgy photo showed a man escaping JW's office building through a fire escape the night Hurtz was slain. Cameras captured the same man loitering at the shopping center parking lot. How can we convince a grand jury we've got our perp?" Councell asked.

"Did you hear how she made an influential man cry one second and laugh the next? Who's this evil woman we're hunting, sir?"

"The answers to your questions are an arm's length away, son."

Blundell stretched an arm through the window and goggled at it.

Fucking comic, Councell thought.

▲ ▲ ▲

Illisya and JW donned shorts, T-shirts, and tennis shoes, and traveled 50 yards from the surveillance van to a nearby park. They joined a soccer game already in progress. Illisya flowed with the wind, intercepted the ball, dribbled, and took a shot at goal. A tentative JW hovered near the touchline.

"Get it, JW."

Illisya passed the ball to him. A girl tackled it away, dribbled, and kicked it up the field.

Councell and Blundell scrutinized Illisya through field glasses as she bought two bottles of water from a vendor. Bailey, a seven-year-old boy, chased Juliet, six, and the girl fell hard. Illisya lifted Juliet and comforted her like a mother as Bailey, mesmerized by the beautiful woman, waited awkwardly.

"Are you sure we're on the right girl? This one is beautiful and compassionate," Blundell said.

"You're looking at an MSV at work."

"What's an MSV?"

"A millennium supervillain, a butcher of four or more. Is she beautiful and compassionate enough for you?"

"So, you think she's a drag on beauty?" Blundell asked.

Councell hammered the steering wheel in frustration.

"I know she's a murderer, and after over a year, I don't have enough evidence to question her," Councell said.

He put away his field glasses.

"The days of ugly, clumsy criminals are fading fast," Blundell said.

"What do you mean?"

"We can't pick up the usual suspect anymore and build cases like back in the day. DNA fucked that ride to hell."

"Is working for the money a terrible thing?" Councell asked.

"We'll have to work triple time to derail soon to be Mrs. Dawes," Blundell said.

Councell flashed an eye toward Illisya.

"The fucking gold-digging whore is too good. She tossed away the last remnants of her crimes," Councell said.

"I'm allergic to everything that grows and crawls in forests," Blundell said.

"Make haste to your vet immediately."

"I'm a horrible snorer too, man."

"Bears get off on shit like that, I heard," Councell said.

"Let's pinch and hold her ass on suspicion."

"Does she look like Sandra Bland to you?" Councell asked.

"My retired grandfather said they used to arrest Blacks, Browns, and trailer trash and fill in the blanks," Blundell said.

"She walked away from the trailer a long time ago and never looked back," Councell said.

Councell sighed.

"I'm not saying my grandfather was right," Blundell added.

Blundell sank back in his seat, apprehensive about a trip to the mountains, his anger toward Illisya rising to unprofessional levels.

There are games to watch, billion-dollar apps to build, and women to chase. A girl as beautiful and intelligent as Illisya Haynes should've married a European prince or built AI platforms in Silicon Valley. Instead, she committed crimes and dragged him from his comfort zone into bear and snake pits. He had never camped and always told enthusiasts: "I'll have what's left when you return."

I'm not a coward but a lover, and performed best in warm, dry places.

"Boss, how massive are fucking Venus's flytraps?"

Councell glanced at him, lost between purgatory and infinity, counting red pebbles on a yellow brick road.

"The department is gonna miss you," Councell said.

"What, you don't believe I'm gonna survive the mountains?"

Councell grinned at him.

A couple of days later, Illisya picked up supplies at a camping gear outlet, and the two detectives approached her from behind shopping trolleys.

"Excuse me, Miss Haynes," Councell said.

Illisya smiled like a church girl receiving the gospel.

"Can I help you, sir?"

"I'm Detective Sergeant Councell, and this is my partner, Blundell."

"How can I help you, detectives?"

"We're investigating the Dawes murders," Blundell said.

"We're sure you'll be able to help us."

"Do you know Mr. Dawes?" Blundell asked.

"Of course. He's a close friend of mine."

"Can you account for your movements last September nineteenth?" Councell asked.

Illisya laughed, threw her head back, and carried it for two minutes more.

"Why would I keep an account of my days and nights from six, nine, ten, twelve fucking months back?"

"Councell, she doesn't have an alibi."

Illisya smiled across her trolley into Blundell's face.

Blundell lost focus, his mind drifting beyond paradise. Yes, I would punish her on our first date. Oh, yeah, I'd take her to the Beach, and after, her nearness inflated my ego to the consistency of Hawaii's Kilauea volcano explosion. I'd bring her home and love her for the remaining days of the universe. Yeah, the fucking beautiful, innocent-looking exterminator hit you like blue skies and warm days in mid-winter. Fuck, did she have a moment with me a second ago, or washed over by Me? I hope she's aware I'm wealthy and my sole purpose out here is to slam the anvil on dirtbags. Illisya's smooth voice brought him back from out there.

"I'm not sure why the fuck I'd need an alibi for back when Jesus walks," Illisya snapped.

She pushed her cart away and turned after ten yards.

"Does my ass move like Sandra Bland's did? When one is guilty, all of you guys should bear the blame."

Blundell and Councell's eyes tagged her as she disappeared into the camping gear department.

Their anger and the proximity of a gorgeous, evil woman left them silent for thirty minutes, buried in thoughts they wished God do not intercept.

Illisya wanted to pump a fist, but professionalism held her arm back and kept her from jumping and clicking her heels. Finally, phase three officially began the moment the Detectives accosted her, and she exhaled a ton of spent-up tension.

Chapter 26

JW and Illisya ate a quiet candlelight dinner at a Polynesian restaurant on the South Beach Strip. As they strutted through the golden crowd in their galaxy for two, Illisya pinched herself at the promises the date night held and glowed inside. She anticipated a pleasant evening, as any Regina could produce, and more. JW nodded or returned waves from business associates and acquaintances. Nevertheless, folks kept their distance.

Illisya took in every minor detail around her. Not one whisper or sly smile passed her as she devoured her lobster Iguru. Her broad-eyed vision captured everything in a single, unblinking glance and stored the details in her brain. Illisya's astute senses would make her a superspy for any of the world's top agencies.

She sipped her Spottswood Cabernet Sauvignon '97 and noticed an old-money couple turn down their faces like the underside of a flowerpot that wintered outside. She drank red wine, whether she ate sea or space food, and relished the freedom to flaunt her audacity anywhere at any time.

However, where is my invitation to move into the mansion? His nonaction there needled my palate in an unconsecrated manner.

The future cometh on a furious path, but girls sometimes get anxious in the middle of an expensive meal.

She tried to recall which of the fucking pessimistic soothsayer poets wrote those words anyway. They should stick to daffodils in Green Glens or fucking elsewhere.

She has never asked him about the interior of the mansion. Still, she suspected most of it was covered with marble, and crystal or gold chandeliers hanging like trumpet flowers in the Celestial garden. Fuck, what are you thinking up there? Oh, well, they lost more in Jack O'Spade than me, for he was a Bible-carrying Christian. What can they expect of me? I've never voluntarily stepped into a church.

JW caught the momentary wrinkle as it fled across Illisya's cool, happy façade.

"What churned in your head, hon? I'm the broken one," JW said.

"A fool in deep thought, ugly, doesn't it."

JW's eyes warmed around the edges, and she pounced.

"What type of music do you dance to, babes?"

"Please don't further break me before I'm mended?" JW asked.

"Your condition called for some drums and bass."

JW sighed and shook his head, but Illisya knew every spot on the beach where he and Regina partied until the night mewled for relief from their light feet.

"Let's go haunt a few of the crowded floors, JW."

"I swore you wanted to dance."

"There you go jumping off conclusion's edge," Illisya said.

JW squinted his eyes into slits at her, and they laughed on cue.

▲ ▲ ▲

Illisya pulled JW onto the Treehouse's dance floor at 2:00 a.m., their fourth stop, after they wandered from one joint to another like a vibe in search of a soul. Regina was a connoisseur of the wild, heavy beats. He danced on Illisya from behind across the floor and wrapped his arms around her waist, losing himself in the music. She bent forward and gyrated her butt on him by moving from the waist in a tight circle. Illisya turned, placed both arms on his shoulders, bubbled before him, and they danced for thirty minutes nonstop.

But guilt visited JW's legs, and he missed a step. What if he revealed too much and ejected Regina's essence from his being?

Over his misgivings, the infectious beats, Illisya's moves, and her smiles pulled him back into the night's warm embrace. Illisya felt the break in concentration and blamed an errant Regina recollection for it.

The following two hours fled by like an illusion under the strobe lights, sprinkled with gold and transformed hair colors and facial features. Yet, by miracle, they reached home and fell asleep by 4:30 a.m.

Fifteen minutes after JW closed his eyes, he dreamed of a beautiful woman who pulled him away from a clear blue river. He wanted to ask her why she had pulled him away, but, as if by magic, she explained that the moment a person entered the river, it would rise and become dangerous. JW and the woman made love in a strange shabby blue bedroom, and he didn't know how they got there. Halfway through, he found out he bedded the wrong woman and not his girl.

He woke, startled, and the proud owner of a palm tree type boner. He grabbed it to ensure he returned from Rainbow's ends and out of ambiguous dreams.

Oh yes, I'm awake.

Illisya slumbered at peace beside him, and nature called him to the bowl.

JW attended a late business dinner two nights later. At 10:00 p.m., Illisya perched in front of her mirror in panties and a bra. Bob Dylan's "Desolation Row" played in the living room, the volume not high enough to impede the planted government devices. The soft light reflected in her eyes, enhancing an intense glow. She gathered her hair, smirked, admired her reflection, and narrowed her eyes.

Illisya smiled at her war face in the mirror and wondered if people looked at attractive evil people the same way they did unattractive ones.

The phone rang and interrupted her.

"Hello, Kali."

"What time are you leaving in the morning?"

"Early, I guess."

"Can we hit the clubs tonight?"

"I crave loud music and smelly people too, at the Hardy Hogg. But I need to get a good night's sleep."

"I love you, Illisya. I'll see you when you return. Watch out for the creepy crawlers in there."

"We're booked at the Burgess. There are no creepy crawlers there, thank you."

"Is that the mountain forest?"

"Good night, Kali. I love you too."

"I'm serious, please be careful."

"Where's your man?"

"At his boys and the game across town, I believe."

"Men, you should get more into sport."

Illisya cut the call, closed her eyes in reflection, and a sad expression overtook her face.

▲ ▲ ▲

The surveillance team in front of Illisya's apartment savored a quiet night in their Williamson Plumbing van as Illisya turned in for the evening. Dread wore an NFL number thirty-three jersey over a hoodie and oversized flame-pattern jeans, jigged, and sang in a perfect Jamaican accent close to the police surveillance van. He stopped, pulled up his pants beside the vehicle, and the unseen officer's nimble fingers touched his service firearm.

"She's all I've got. She's my safe love. She's all I need. She's my safe love. There are no fears to kill my vibes when I'm at her side. She's my safe love waiting home, with safe love for me."

He strolled away, buried his hands in his pockets, caught a bus, rode for a mile, and got off at the Hardy Hoggs Pub at Biscayne and Flagler. He tossed his keys from one hand to the other, approached a row of bikes, sat on a green dirt bike, fired the motor, and juiced the accelerator. Rodents bolted into the drain as he donned his helmet, revved the engine, and sped away.

▲ ▲ ▲

Dread throttled in front of a house on SW 12th Terrace, a mahogany-lined residential thoroughfare in the Brickell neighborhood. He scrolled to the game on his phone for a minute, dismounted, and knocked on a side door. Kali opened the door.

"Is the game over already? And where is your key?"

He brushed past Kali as if demons were chasing him.

The song "One Day in the City" jammed on the stereo, and Kali locked the door. He shot her four times as she moved back from the door and dropped the gun. The killer cradled Kali's head in his lap, rocked back and forth, and cried rivers of tears.

"Oh, Kali, you were my only friend, and you've lost the bet we made years ago without a memory of the wager."

The disguised Illisya dabbed her eyes.

"Why did you wander off into experts and their negative territories? You went in too far, babes. I could never get you back. I'm so sorry, my friend, but how could I let you meet my JW?"

Illisya rocked back and forth in mental agony, Kali's head in her arms, and tears ran down her synthetic cheeks.

"I'm sorry. I suspected I might have to do this to you from that night in Negril. I honestly wished it didn't have to happen, but your mouth."

She dabbed at Kali's face, eased her head to the floor, and replaced her helmet.

Minutes later, the disguised Illisya parked the bike at the Hardy Hogg, tied the helmet to the seat, and hailed a cab. She entered through the southern entrance of her building, away from the surveillance van, slipped through a service entrance, and ran up the stairs. She shredded her disguise, packed away a small bag inside her backpack, and placed it beside the other camping gear five minutes before JW and Van Drake arrived.

They rode north on 27th Avenue and took 36th Street to the airport. JW spent the ride on his tablet, tying up last-minute work details. Illisya relaxed in her seat, a hand on JW's leg, and smiled when he turned his face, but didn't want to interrupt him further.

Give them hell for our money, babes. It won't be long now. She whispered in her heart.

Chapter 27

Crispy morning fog and mist fought the rising sun for sole possession of the Chattahoochee National Park staging area. Insects and birds piped their displeasure as an SUV intruded on their peace. The morning after Kali's murder, Illisya jumped from the driver's side of the vehicle, bounced on her toes, and held her face to the heavens. She squinted against the early rays and inhaled lungs full of unpolluted air.

"How do you see me as a free-will practitioner from up there? The news said your secret heavenly outposts went underground to avoid NASA's probes."

An apprehensive JW stepped from the vehicle, stretched his muscles, and eyed the mountain with trepidation.

When Illisya woke him hours ago, he wanted to abort and fly back home. However, he had come this far and was not a quitter. Nevertheless, he gazed at the hill and yearned for his warm hotel bed. Illisya encircled his waist with an arm and held his hand.

"Hey, I'll be there with you," Illisya assured.

He smiled at her.

"Why do you think I shook in my damn boots?"

Illisya wrapped her arms around him, gazed into his face, and smiled softly as a butterfly landed on a red, life-giving cup of nectar in the light breeze. Last night, JW brought bliss, and her expectations bubbled like the new, untamed morning. Illisya conjured a place where they would make love on the leaves and readied herself to squeeze juicy bonuses from wayward dreams.

"Something tells me not to believe you," Illisya said.

She tipped forward, and JW kissed her.

Illisya, Mr. Hayne, and Bill visited the park twice, and she rode up solo two months before she met JW and charted a course. JW's private jet landed at Fulton County Airport-Brown Field on a trip that epitomized a journey in class minus good intentions.

▲ ▲ ▲

By 10:00 a.m., Illisya labored uphill under her pack inside the park. Dense wilderness flanked the trail on both sides, and JW swore he heard smooth critters purring on his left, right, and above, like when his Bentley throttled.

"Why do I always lead?" Illisya asked.

"For inducement, I guess."

"Where's my mini skirt when I need it?"

"It'd work as well. Who taught you your bushcraft?"

"Dad did, before he went AWOL years ago. He was a Green Beret who warped into a spook and came home as a mercenary."

"You've never spoken much about your folks."

"After he dumped mother our relationship galloped downhill in an unstoppable spiral."

"I'm sorry. So did your father teach you bear craft or bear wrestling?"

"Why?"

"It may be nothing, but a huge ugly bear followed us for the last five minutes."

Illisya parted a tree branch, gawked down the track, and an enormous black bear waddled uphill.

"Oh, I read somewhere they're harmless from two hundred yards or more."

"Let's hold our advantage," JW said.

They hurried over the crest, down the slope, and ducked into the shrubbery.

The bear shuffled, sniffed the air, stopped where the lovers left the trail, and towered on its hind legs. A sizable branch popped, fell, and crashed behind the animal. It shuffled off at a trot into the underbrush away from JW and Illisya.

Illisya sat on a log and laughed beneath the canopy, while JW stood, shaken.

"What's so amusing about being mauled?"

"Not mauled, and the rush jumped right in front of me, honey. Where else but the great outdoors could we get such a rush?" Illisya asked.

"Did I tell you about the day I scared the rain back?"

"I'm a wind chaser myself. We zoomed beyond the rain and spread our dreams. But in love, we're soft to the touch."

Illisya kissed JW.

She buried her face in JW's chest, her right fist tightening and releasing as if molding playdough.

If she could've, she would've shouted it, you're my love, and I wouldn't even gloat, for my coup de grâce rises around the corner, more impressive than a blue moon on a cloudless night.

▲ ▲ ▲

A camouflaged sniper scrambled up a white ash one hundred and fifty feet away. His taut arms and facial skin had the consistency of carved, sun-cured hides. Hard lines suggested he touched sixty and left it in his dust years back. Nimbleness insulated his age, and inflexible skin cut sharp trenches around cunning eyes. An M2010 ESR rifle rested across his shoulders as he settled between two limbs and surveyed the woods through field glasses.

His lenses found Councell and Blundell under the shrubbery, ragged in appearance, as if the forest had hiked them instead of the other way around.

The man chuckled at what the woodlands did to people who circled parking lots five times searching for spots near entrances, where they could piss into buildings from their vehicles. His scope found JW and noted how his eyes celebrated Illisya's glow and closeness as it diluted his anxiety edges. The sniper's actions unfolded as if he woke every morning to stalk campers and hold their lives on a whim. He could shoot them as easily as peeing on a bush, and the intensity in his eyes said as much. He settled so well into the foliage that a bird landed a foot from him.

▲ ▲ ▲

The trees creaked from a gust of wind above Illisya and JW. He cocked an ear, brow furrowed, and listened to the untapped, uncontrollable energy overhead.

Fallen trees smashed onto people's houses. Nevertheless, every nerve in his body welcomed nature's voices.

Illisya tugged at his lapel, and a carnal twinkle crossed her eyes.

"Where did you come across David and his syndrome?" JW asked.

"In college, I don't quite remember."

"What about Joseph's syndrome?"

"Who's he?" Illisya asked.

"A fellow whose cute coat landed him in trouble and legend. Joseph's beautiful suit led to David's crown and syndrome."

"Your Joseph sure doesn't sound like he played a lot to me."

"I want to be your Joseph, if you'll have me," JW said.

"I'm light years ahead of you. I still wonder sometimes if you've ever thought of doing it in the jungle."

"No, I've never thought about it."

"You've never sat in your office, let your mind fly, and bent a hot gal over a log among these giants?" Illisya asked.

"It's inconceivable I missed something so mundane, isn't it?"

"Well, Mr. Curving Imagination, sir. We're on a log, and I'm a hot gal."

She planted an enthusiastic kiss on his lips and squeezed his nipple.

▲ ▲ ▲

JW stoked a fire beside their tent between trees in the late evening. Crickets, frogs, toads, and other forest denizens tossed shots at each other's bows as sunrays withdrew from between the trees. A stream trickled nearby. Illisya approached camp with a tote bag, squatted beside JW, and massaged the back of his neck.

"Hmm, I could grow to love whatever you're doing to my neck."

"How about a month in the Amazon rainforest?"

"Some of us will laugh, and others will cry and die first," JW said.

"Okay lets hit, Kali's boyfriend's ganja farm in the hills of western Jamaica will do."

JW turned an amused eye, and they laughed together.

"So, you crossed a stream, climbed an hour between massive rock formations, admired wildflowers and orchids, swatted a zillion mosquitoes, and you're right there," Illisya said.

JW laughed until his eyes teared up.

"I'm allergic to chikungunya mosquitoes," JW said.

"No, they ply their seasonal trade in the cities."

They bantered, roasted corn on the cob, and ate juicy tomatoes with crackers. After two hours of wordplay, Illisya yawned, stood, and stretched.

"Let's get a jump on tomorrow," Illisya said.

Before JW reacted, she raced into the shelter like a playful child.

▲ ▲ ▲

A Mischief of bush rats emerged in the still night, rummaging and nibbling crumbs around the dying fire.

The sniper crept toward the campsite, his shooter aimed at the tent, eyes fixed on the flap. Twigs popped, and the rodents scurried past him. Six rats dashed toward him. He jumped, and they bolted between his legs. The gunman slunk back like an earthworm and disappeared.

Councell and Blundell sneaked into camp from the opposite direction. Blundell held his sidearm low. They gawked at Illisya and JW's tent for ten minutes and withdrew, clearly not enjoying the trip.

The officers erected their shelters two hundred meters away over a log. Blundell sat on one end and scrolled his phone.

"Wow, they found the Falkner girl dead in her apartment this morning," Blundell said.

"Our girl killed her before she left last night."

"But how? We covered her building until they left for the airport."

Councell bowed his head, struck by an epiphany.

"Fuck, I know what happened to Jack O'Spade. Remember the beheaded investment banker who floated on a Jamaican beach about a year ago?"

"You're grabbing at straws," Blundell said.

"Text the office. Check if Kali Falkner and Illisya Haynes visited Jamaica at the time and stayed at the same resort as the fellow," Councell said.

Blundell typed for half a minute.

"What do you think happened out there?"

"Jack ran out of luck. I believe he stayed at the same resort as the girls, and Kali Falkner recognized him."

"Who threw the fatal blow?" Blundell asked.

"Our girl, down bush, of course."

"I put the hardware in Mop Stick Dread's hands," Blundell said.

"No. We checked him out. The handsome skinny motherfucker plied his ganja trade at the hotel. The Falkner girl pussy-whipped him, but—"

Blundell's device pinged.

"Ezekiel Callaghan stayed at the same resort as the girls before he lost his head," Blundell said.

"Bill and Kali are dead. If Skinny Dread swung the blade or even dreamed the girls did it, he'd be dead already."

"What now?"

"The wedding is the only thing left on her board. Good night, Blundell."

Councell burrowed into his bag and thought of his wife. She returned to his bed, and a serial killer dragged him into forbidden wilderness among snakes and bugs. When he locked her up, he was going to punch her in the gut and kick her ribs behind thick walls, out of public view.

Blundell listened to the myriad night sounds, his skin crawling. He hoped nothing would target him and brought friends. He majored in computer science at FIU as a backup after deciding to be a cop at ten, on his first ride in his grandfather's squad car.

His grandfather, a burly outdoor patrol sergeant, left an eternal impression when he took down a rowdy punk fist for fist. His father was a soccer nut and a retired civil engineer. His mother retired from city management two years ago, and they now haunt beaches and sunny destinations worldwide.

Blundell made his first million at 18, bought a house, and converted half of it into an extended AI lab. He sold a small security patch app six months ago for his first sale and kept churning zeros toward his next global monster.

He fancied himself a flamboyant Tony Stark, drove cool cars, built high-tech devices, and solved crimes. He also carried the second male manhood, the big iron beneath his two-thousand-dollar suits.

"At times, Heaven gets impatient, and it comes to a fellow."

He fitted earplugs, removed them, and listened. He wanted to hear if animals or a certain killer girl came in the night.

At 4:00 a.m., nature called him from a dream best described as a dark fantasy prompt. He kept guard until sunrise.

Chapter 28

Sunrays muscled through the shrubberies, and the forest's denizens chattered in strange tongues. JW appeared in the morning sunlight and straightened his wrinkled arms above his head. He stretched sleepy muscles, and by his expression, they popped back into place, alien to him. Illisya splashed about in the stream.

He parted the branches and gawked as Illisya swam in a clear pool of water. She giggled at him and mounted a rock, the same rock she stood on when she felt Bill's eyes on her eight years ago. She appreciated his eyes on other occasions. However, on that day, she didn't want him to see her fit a menstrual cup.

"Good morning, hon," Illisya said.

JW glowed.

"Hello, Mrs. Dawes."

"I do love the ring Mrs. Dawes brings. But please knock the next time you enter the bathroom. I could've been, you know, not decent."

Illisya contorted, twisted, and toweled. JW's face opened, and the joyous flame burned away the nuisances.

"Forgive me, but the breakfast issue dangled in the morning like rust," JW said.

"It's entirely up to you, but you can bet your life it will not be leftovers."

JW's eyes twinkled.

After instant coffee, hard bagels, and boiled eggs, JW and Illisya broke down camp and trekked up a steep footpath by 8:00 a.m.

Mist covered the valley behind them like a still ocean as they reached the peak and traveled downhill on the other side. JW's head pivoted toward where forest denizens dropped new melodies. Illisya grinned at him from behind and hoped she hadn't plunged a city guy into something too overwhelming for his senses. JW ducked as a woodpecker nailed a tree above his head, and Illisya stifled a laugh.

Morning golden sun shafts penetrated the canopies and pumped energy into a once lethargic JW. Illisya kept pace, a million thoughts about the mansion running through her mind. JW hit a fork, braked, and she bumped into him on purpose.

Illisya frowned at the well-trodden left fork that led into a valley and pointed at the right, to an overgrown, cobweb-laced track. A gust of wind barged through the trees and popped limbs. A flock of rose-breasted grosbeaks took off to a quieter neighborhood from human intruders and noisy winds.

"Don't you think we'd flip a coin?" JW asked.

Illisya pointed down the well-trodden path.

"Let's avoid city traffic and head for the sticks, I say."

JW widened his eyes at her.

"Why, I'm not surprised."

"Do you want me to lead?" Illisya asked.

"The clean air has revived something in me. I should return to my mental and physical peak in a day or two."

"God help me."

He flicked his head and used his stick to clear cobwebs along the downhill track. After an hour, a swift, broad river roared to their right, and thick woods bordered the left.

"Did we hit the Mississippi?" JW asked.

"Don't ever compare a gutter to the mighty Mississippi."

"Are you sure it's not a small sea?"

"I'm not laughing."

They ambled single file through a footpath reclaimed by young growth, the river roaring to their right.

"In another thirty minutes, we set camp and break out the fishing lines," Illisya said.

"If we don't catch anything?"

"These fish cooperated with me in the past, hon."

"The jar of Jamaican jerk seasoning is for fish not caught?"

"You're twice a genius, sir."

They reached Illisya's campsite from her recon mission. JW picked up an old piece of firewood and inspected it.

"This is not so old."

"My Father, Bill, and I trudged through here like ten years ago."

She had also camped there shortly before she met JW. At night, she sneaked out the back of her tent armed and slept in a tree to her left. She called it a lone woman's precaution in the sticks.

Illisya paused, glanced behind her, listened, ran, and tapped JW on the shoulder. He turned. She pressed a finger to her lips, and he tiptoed closer. She held his arm and pointed behind her.

"I think we're being followed," Illisya said.

Illisya expected Councell and Blundell to follow her to the mountains and had spotted them hiding in a hotel nook the night they checked in, like rats. She doubted the officers knew she fed them the hotel name through their bugs. Fuck, imagine the dash they made to reach it before us. She might be the death of the two fine officers as they matched their free will against hers. She glowed inside. Nevertheless, she had to tolerate them, for they were the escape hatch in the grand design trap.

"Who's following us?" JW whispered.

"I don't know. Let's find out."

They ducked behind trees and released their packs. Two minutes later, Councell led Blundell down the track, winded like tired donkeys.

"What's the meaning of this?" JW asked.

Illisya helped him untangle his arm from a strap, and he accosted the two detectives.

Illisya followed him.

"We've got our jobs to do, Mr. Dawes," Councell said.

"Am I a suspect in my family's death?"

"Your family wasn't the only one who got killed," Blundell said.

"Everyone's a suspect," Councell said.

He gazed at Illisya with icy eyes.

"I repeat. No one's above suspicion."

The cops trailed the couple, and the sniper followed them. A flock of birds flew up from feeding ahead. He swung up a tree and spotted the four arguing through his glasses.

Both officers glared at Illisya when a slug zinged by them and struck a massive pine trunk. The report echoed. JW froze as bark chipped inches from his head.

"Take cover," Councell shouted.

Illisya tugged JW's sleeve, and they sprinted behind a humongous oak. They braced their backs against the trunk, away from the shooter, and held each other's hands. Eleven bullets struck the other side of the tree, digging holes where their heads should have been. The officers lay flat behind cover and fired toward the unseen assailant.

The shooter concentrated fire on JW's position, keeping his head pinned. Blundell fired wildly, his AR-15 sounding minuscule against the shooter's weapon.

"Save your bullets," Councell bellowed.

"JW, JW," Illisya screamed.

"Are you hit, darling?" JW asked.

"I don't know. I don't know."

"Crawl away behind the trees and run like hell," Councell said.

They crawled into a thicket and abandoned their packs.

JW, Illisya, Blundell, and Councell ran through the brush to a swift, uncrossable stream. They gawked and ran along the riverbank, sparsely lined with trees.

"JW, there's no cover out here."

"Run for the trees up ahead," Blundell shouted.

▲ ▲ ▲

Back at the ambush point, the brutal gunman rested against a sapling. A police radio squawked from a backpack on the ground. He smashed it and the cell phones, shook an NFL number thirty-three jersey, Dread's mask, and flame-pattern jeans from Illisya's bag.

The man frowned at the mask, turned it on a finger, tossed it onto a pile, and set the bundle on fire. He aimed high and fired six rounds in the general direction the group fled. He poured fuel from a flask onto stubborn pieces, broke branches, and beat out wandering tongues of flame.

▲ ▲ ▲

The wind died, and brilliant sunlight reflected off the water's surface. JW and Illisya huddled behind a giant pine, sweating in the shadows. Councell and Blundell crouched behind separate trees, soaked as if they had swum in their clothes.

Driftwood and trash lodged high in branches above them from times when overflow waters surged through the timber.

"You said you didn't have enemies, Mr. Dawes," Councell said.

"Who said he's mine?"

"You took all the fire back there," Blundell said.

"That's not fair," Illisya said.

"Someone murdered my partner and three other people and is running free. You tell me what's fair," Councell said.

His eyes drilled into Illisya.

"How do you know they're not running straight ahead instead of in a circle?" Illisya asked.

She swatted a bug.

"If you were real detectives, you'd have figured out what they were doing and brought them to justice months ago," she continued.

"Someone will be brought to justice, and soon," Blundell said.

"While you're doing your job, we'll be moving on. Let's go, Illisya," JW said.

JW took Illisya's hand and led her toward the river. She bent a limb to its limit as she followed JW and released it. It snapped back hard enough to knock a man unconscious. She grinned over her shoulder at the officers. Councell touched his weapon and gawked at her with intent. Blundell checked his phone.

"I don't have any signal," Councell said.

"We lost signal when we came down the slope," Blundell said.

"I have a satellite phone in my pack."

"What do you think the man did with it?"

JW and Illisya stood on the riverbank as water crashed against a cliff on the far side.

▲ ▲ ▲

The river bent into a U shape and encircled JW's ticket at the bottom from the POV of the forest's cape. A steep cliff ran along the far bank, and flat land lay on JW's side.

JW and Illisya stared at the swift, angry water.

"I'm afraid we're trapped. The only way out is behind us," JW said.

"Let's go back."

"The cops are behind you."

Both officers stepped forward, frozen between the river's scope and the shooter lurking behind them.

They gazed across the sheer rock face on the far side.

"It's impossible to cross," Councell said.

"We're going to die here. I don't want to die, and it's my fault," Illisya screamed.

She paced in panic. JW embraced her.

"Listen to me, honey. We're going to be fine, and it's not your fault," JW assured her.

Blundell glanced at Councell, and they both gave Illisya an 'oh, please' look.

Two shots echoed, and hot slugs whistled through the trees. Illisya screamed and bolted from JW's arms. The rifle thundered, and tracers buzzed past.

JW chased her down, grabbed her arm, slowed her, and they crawled back between the massive trunks. Illisya sobbed against his shoulder as he rubbed her back.

"He's going to get us," Illisya cried.

"Please be quiet, honey. I'll get us out of here."

Councell crawled between covers, and Blundell joined him.

"The bitch is good," Blundell said.

"Here's my question. Is Killer Girl better than us at her job?" Councell asked.

"I'm not sure anymore, and I'm scared to ask who fed my phone signal to the fish," Blundell said.

"Scuttle up a tall tree."

"You never did answer me when I asked how many partners you've been through," Blundell said.

Councell crawled closer to JW, hating the thought of another night in the wilderness.

Meanwhile, dark clouds rolled across the sky miles upriver and broke into a monsoon. Rain fell like the deluge men wrote about from time immemorial. Lightning pulsed. Thunder shook the world as water poured its spite onto the land. The mother river thundered as tributaries churned muddy waters into its body.

Chapter 29

JW, Councell, Blundell, and Illisya crouched behind sturdy trees, trapped and expecting the worst. Blundell pulled down a piece of driftwood, and old, washed debris fell on him.

"The area floods constantly," Blundell said.

"Well, let's pray it doesn't rain," Councell said.

Six shots barked, and bullets whistled through the leaves. Flocks of birds soared in circles, cawed, returned, and took off at the next barrage.

"Stay down. He's waiting for us to break cover," Councell said.

Blundell and Councell made themselves small as the midday sun hovered overhead as if searching under the trees for them.

Years ago, Illisya carved *Billy Boy Peeks and Wishes* on a water oak trunk. She glanced up at her artwork above her head, bolted in a panic, and screamed at the top of her voice.

"No, Illisya," JW shouted.

JW chased her, and the detectives followed as she ran thirty yards and fell on purpose. A tremor ran through her body. She should've erased the heart on her last recon trip. What if he suspected she led him there? Her work had progressed too far to fail due to a simple error.

She shuddered in his arms at the thought, and JW mistook it for anxiety over the unknown shooter.

Van Drake wanted to shadow JW with two men, and JW insisted he should not. As shots echoed and Illisya trembled in his arms, it dawned on him that he may have made an error. They would've had his back and neutralized the threat quietly. Hell, hardened professionals like him shouldn't make so many simple mistakes. He patted Illisya's head and played with her hair.

▲ ▲ ▲

Minutes dragged into hours. JW leaned back against a beechwood trunk, and Illisya's head rested in his lap. Blundell lay flat on his stomach, and Councell peeked into the sun at the edge of the western horizon.

"He's been quiet for over an hour. I think he's gone," Blundell said.

"No, he's out there. I can feel it," Councell said.

"The water sounds different to me."

"It's just the wind."

Illisya raised her head.

"Yes, it definitely sounds different."

"Oh shit, I know why he stopped shooting. It's the river," JW said.

"What do you mean?" Councell asked.

"Oh my God, we're about to be flooded out," Illisya cried.

They gaped at the washing limbs as floodwater added a new twist of apprehension. Illisya searched for a sapling suitable to climb in the coming dark.

▲ ▲ ▲

The sniper stooped and crushed a piece of cigar into the soil as the mighty deluge rushed six yards away. He marveled at Mother Nature's power and how puny human endeavors were against its fury. It reminded him of ten runaway trains side by side as they smashed everything in their path and left destruction in their wake.

Water crashed against the cliff, splashed back into the thicket, and drove fear into the strongest hearts.

"Can the ocean accommodate all this water?"

He turned, squeezed off a couple of rounds at ground level, and lit a cigar. The water surged through the ticket eight feet high by the time he burned the smelly thing.

▲ ▲ ▲

JW and Illisya perched high on a limb together and clung like awkward monkeys. Blundell and Councell hung in separate trees, a million miles out of their elements. Visibility dropped to a yard or two, and the water roared through the ticket like thunder on a front lawn.

Illisya shouted above the roar.

"My feet are getting wet, JW."

"If we climb any higher, we'll touch the blasted moon," Councell said.

"I'm wet too. Let's touch the moon," JW said.

"Please keep your voices down," Councell said.

"He can't hear us over the water," JW said.

"It's my fault. I shouldn't have taken you out here," Illisya said.

"Don't blame yourself. You couldn't have known this would happen."

JW scrambled up a couple of limbs, and Illisya followed.

"As I recuperated from the miracles of Mother Nature's healing hands, the madman showed," JW said.

"Or madwoman," Illisya said.

"Oh my God. Carol or Tiffany."

"Who are they?" Illisya asked.

JW's brow furrowed. Illisya turned her face away and smiled. If she could, she would've run a victory lap.

"What is it, baby?" Illisya asked.

"I'm such a fool. I shouldn't have missed it."

Illisya shrieked, and JW rubbed her shoulders.

"Please don't fall apart," JW said.

Rats squeaked between the trees.

"Vermin," Blundell bellowed.

"I can't see them," Councell said.

"They're climbing the trees," JW said.

Blundell ripped off a branch and swatted the rodents.

"Beat them off with a branch," Councell said.

JW tore a branch, split it in two, and handed one piece to Illisya.

▲ ▲ ▲

As hide sites go, the rifleman built his in plain sight, constructed of wood high on two branches. The moon hung on a long string, and he didn't anticipate return fire as he drank casually from a flask. He shuffled into position, raised the night scope, and tagged JW's upper body high in a crook.

A finger curled around the trigger and lingered. The man inhaled, steadied his hands, moved the crosshair to Councell's right shoulder, and squeezed the trigger. The detective yelled as the bullet's impact knocked him into the water.

▲ ▲ ▲

Councell shouted in agony, floated, and the current flipped him face down.

"Sarge, fuck no," Blundell shouted.

A bullet whistled past him, and he squeezed himself against the tree.

Illisya jumped into the water, swam Councell down, and rolled him. The flow carried them between saplings. She grabbed at a limb, missed, and slammed between two trunks.

Illisya braced her back, slipped her arms under Councell's shoulders, and wedged his head above water between the trees.

The flood worked like an oiled cog in her machine, a gift she couldn't have planned in a million years.

"Help, will someone help me here?" Illisya shouted.

JW and Blundell flinched as slugs nailed wood around them.

"Jump, JW, jump," Illisya shouted.

Blundell lost his balance and fell.

"Holy hell."

JW barely saw Illisya but heard her cries and jumped. A slug struck the spot as he left it. The water swept him away. He grabbed for a branch, missed, slammed into another, and clung to a smaller one.

Councell coughed up water, sucked air into his lungs, and twisted to face Illisya.

"You're smart and a fucking clever criminal. Saving me doesn't change my opinion of you."

"What's your opinion of me? Do you think I wear dirty underwear?"

"You know what I meant. You're not getting away with four murders."

"I suppose you've heard of the theory of everything."

"Enlighten me," Councell said.

"It's the concept of an invisible chain connecting humanity. When society fails to right wrongs, it breeds super ass villains like your murderers on the margins."

"Can your hypothesis convince a jury? I don't have murderers. I have you."

Illisya giggled.

"My defense? How will you manage a court appearance with zero evidence against me?"

"You're trapped inside your own evil head," Councell said.

"Put it down as the day cable news spoke false truth to wild winds and realities crashed and burned."

"Good God, are you political too?"

"If the president can claim he's a genius, why not?" Illisya asked.

"I want you to know, before I lock you away on death row, I agreed with you on the moron genius thing."

Illisya smiled, one of her sweetest, right in his face.

"Mr. I've never worn dirty underwear, hold it together and run. You've got nothing else coming," Illisya whispered.

Councell coughed up a mouthful of dirty water.

Fuck, what would a jury think without hard evidence after hearing she risked her life to save mine? I need divine help to put her away.

"I bet we're on the same plane of thought here, Detective," Illisya said.

"Blundell, where are you? Come and get me," Councell called, coughing again.

Chapter 30

The gunman unfurled his sleeping bag, lay on his back, and folded his arms.

Blundell and JW held Councell in a cluster of branches, and Illisya tied his shirt with a belt over his wound. As crazy nights go, the gunfire and the flood dragged on in the thicket without further incident, and by dawn the water receded, leaving mud everywhere.

At 5:00 a.m., the sniper packed his kit, climbed down, and withdrew into the vast wilderness. Birds rose with the sun, marauded through the woods without fear or bounds, pecked at each other, and cawed. The world opened its doors for business, and the air of survival and mud smelled fresh.

JW, Illisya, and the two men huddled in knee-deep mud, and Councell nursed his injured shoulder in a makeshift sling.

"Is he still out there?" Illisya asked.

"He's been quiet for hours," JW said.

"Someone will have to try to get help," Councell said.

"I'll go back up the hill until I find reception," Blundell said.

Blundell crept away, eyes darting, his hand steady on his pistol. He reached the original ambush point, saw the broken satellite phone, and his hope was dashed.

A twig broke. Blundell pulled his firearm, whipped his head to the right, saw nothing, ran, and a deer sprinted the other way behind him.

▲ ▲ ▲

At midday, EMS helped Councell into a helicopter. JW dodged reporters and ushered Illisya into a second hired craft.

Late that evening, the sniper exited I-75 at exit 256, driving an everyman pickup truck. He pumped gas at a station, gazed west at a motel's neon light, and hardened his already iron façade.

Chapter 31

Three months after the mountain caper, a gray pest control car painted like a giant rodent cut off Illisya's car and sped up Biscayne Avenue. Illisya braked, her tires squealed, and she hit her horn as she pulled into a pharmacy parking lot. The past three months wore the camping disaster down to dust in her memory.

JW ogled her calm demeanor from the passenger seat. He would have flown into a rage if someone had cut him off.

"Are you coming?"

"I'll wait here for you and catch up on some paperwork," JW said.

She kissed him and hurried into the pharmacy, a gigantic diamond weighing down her ring finger.

JW admired her butt as she danced away, a husband in love. Illisya turned, blew a kiss, and he laughed. Sometimes, he felt ashamed to love her more or as much as he did Regina.

Illisya pushed a trolley down the aisle, and Mr. Haynes, the sniper, cheapened an already wrinkled gray suit and bumped it. She didn't make eye contact as her father read a label.

"Did you have to be so fucking realistic, Dad?"

A smile tried to soften Mr. Haynes's face and failed.

"Didn't you want to get off what's his name's most suspected person list?" Mr. Haynes asked.

"Yeah, yet I didn't want you to kill us dead."

"When I want to murder people, they're dead. You're squeamish like your running ass mother. And I don't have the ability to flood rivers either."

"It turned out to be a gift for us."

Illisya smiled at his stern face.

"Where's Mom, by the way?"

"I'm not with lost and found."

"That I forgot."

Illisya knew he lied.

"Are you still the suspect?"

"Oh yes, the courts can't convict me now. You're gonna be a granddad too," Illisya quipped.

"Great news for you and the millionaire. What I want you to do is deliver his money."

"Billionaire, not million. Let me hear you moan about not having a son now and blame it on Mother."

Illisya poked him with a finger.

"No fucking son of yours could've done better."

"Do you know how long a son can stay in the field without..."

Mr. Haynes grabbed canned food by the dozens.

"The paper said your wedding rivaled anything Miami saw in the last ten years. It's such a shame your parents are dead or something."

"You came without invitation in disguise. I searched like hell and couldn't identify you. Did you kill someone and attend as them?"

Illisya dropped a box of cough syrup into her cart.

"You're one incredibly understanding father at times."

"Daughters deserve nothing less from their parents," Mr. Haynes said.

Illisya fished a fat envelope from her pocketbook and tossed it into his cart.

"A hundred thousand, a small sample of what's to come. Nice chatting. We bagged a good one. Years of sacrifice and planning paved our future green."

"I miss Billy Boy," Mr. Haynes said.

"Collateral damage. Did you know Bill used to peek at me while I washed on our camping trips?"

"I hate sissies. I would've plugged him if he hadn't. Say hello to the old woman for me."

"To hear from the likes of you would be detrimental to her wellbeing, and you know how I've loved her from birth."

Illisya pushed her cart away, and he stared after her, a proud father.

She sold him the general outline of her plan while he hunted terrorists in Latvia. It sounded dubious at the sale, but she filled in the holes over the years, and he bought the heist of the century. Years ago, she told him they would communicate in code through the police bugs when they installed them in her apartment.

The operation forced him to disappear for years, a natural trait for him, an invisible shadow from early youth. He temporarily dumped his wife, a straightforward business decision to him. He accused the poor woman of infidelity, drove the fear of death into her, and made her run as part of the job.

That night on the phone, Illisya told him to drive her away, and he didn't mince words about what would happen when he got home. His tone did the job.

She cheated in their early years together, and he married her one year later as an unfaithful man himself. He couldn't blame her for what he indulged in day and night on the job worldwide. Fairness to women may have been the only decent quality the man possessed, and he hated it when work dictated the eradication of a female.

His DNA result on Illisya at six months old returned positive, and he showed no further interest in what his wife did or didn't do. Notwithstanding being a killer for hire, he avoided giving anyone a burden he wouldn't carry himself.

Mr. Haynes rushed the bike to the Hardy Hogg Pub when Illisya mentioned the name in her bedroom. She worked out the minutest details years ago, even the secret color they would use as markers, and he tied the green ribbon to the emerald bike's handle for identification. Mr. Dawes pocketed the envelope.

"My wife remained one of the humblest and most respectful persons in Heaven or Earth, and you don't dump on people like her."

The culmination of the gig included bringing her back into their lives soon. She worked in a casino kitchen in Vegas instead of a classroom. He planned to approach her, bitchy if needed, and explain what color underwear she wore the night she cheated, to convince her it had never been a thing.

The sniper's phone pinged with a text message. It said there's $1 million in your account.

"FM meant Find Mom, I guess. I already knew where she lived and worked, and I don't mind coming into the light for a Vegas trip."

JW hopped out of the vehicle and helped Illisya unload the contents of her shopping trolley into the trunk.

"I got a hint from the cagey old woman Meg minutes ago," Illisya said.

JW gave her his full attention.

"My Mother called her, and she and Dad may reunite. I'm not supposed to know, and I'm gonna needle every bit of information out of her old butt when I get over there."

"That'd be great, babes. I hope she returns in time to help you with the babies."

"Babies, JW?"

"You should be with child again by this time next year, young lady."

They laughed, and their eyes twinkled.

Chapter 32

Ron danced two steps, raked fallen leaves in Meg's driveway, and sang to himself, his face as cheerful as morning in a marigold field.

"One day in the city is a day in the universe..."

He repeated the line ten times under the noise of the rake and leaves, paused, danced forward, and backed a few steps.

"Heroes returning from battles to die in the Streets, we're living for changes, but changes give no more..."

Illisya drove into the driveway and waited as he scurried out of the way. She cut the ignition, hopped from the car, and left JW inside. Ron smiled at her, sane as the Pope. She lifted grocery bags from the trunk. Ron reached for them. Illisya released the handles. He pulled his hands away, and the bags fell between them.

Illisya glanced down, appalled.

Ron shot her in the upper body three times.

The bullets slammed her against the car, and she slumped dead.

"Illisya, oh my God, no," JW yelled.

Ron's face brightened as if he had accomplished his life's work. He ran around the car to meet JW, held the muzzle of the gun, and pushed the butt into the car window. JW shuffled toward the driver's side, livid.

"Hey, man, come back to your door. It's your turn to play. Take the thing. A day in the city is a day in the universe."

JW struggled out of the car as Ron forced his upper body through the window, the pistol held butt-first toward JW.

"Get away from me," JW bellowed.

JW climbed out, cradled Illisya's head, and wailed on the ground.

"Oh, Illisya, no. Not you too, baby, no. Shoot me also, you murderer. Take my life."

"Hey, why all these ugly connotations? We're on the trip, man, and it's your turn."

"I said murder me also," JW shouted.

JW kissed Illisya's face. Ron sank to his knees and lamented on the other side of the car.

"Man, it's a day in the city. What kind of fool refuses to play on such an ordained day? Fuck if I know what's wrong with people in these cities where we danced and died. Heroes returning from battles to die in the Streets. We lived for changes, but changes give no more. One day in the city is a day in the universe..."

Meg sat in front of the television, sunk back on the sofa with her eyes closed and arms folded, when Illisya pulled into the driveway and tooted her horn. She tried three times to rise, fell back on her butt, gathered her strength, and stood. Her fists tightened on the walker.

The report of three shots followed by JW's anguished cry reached her.

She shambled onto the porch and met JW's shattered eyes and Illisya's head in his lap. Meg clutched her heart. A foot kicked the walker away, and she collapsed in a heap.

▲ ▲ ▲

Councell and Blundell's unmarked car screamed onto the scene from around the corner as if they had set the stage and waited for the trap to spring. The Officers rushed in to collect the spoils. Ron wailed on his knees, oblivious of the cops.

"It's one day in the city, man. Oh, Stacy baby, it's a day in the universe."

Councell cuffed him and gawked at Blundell.

"I told you a god named Karma lived near us," Blundell said.

"You mean a stealer of diligent cops' glory, don't you?" Councell asked.

▲ ▲ ▲

People gathered at the perimeter as medics wheeled Meg toward the ambulance in a body bag. JW held his head and mourned like a soul in a torment in the back of Councell's vehicle.

▲ ▲ ▲

Beyond the police lines, the Sad Bum and the Distinguished Gent leaned against the Bentley. The Gent smiled gleefully into the Bum's face, his eyes intense.

"I trust this little drama proved a point to you and your boss. Free Will warped into an enormous error through the ages," the Gent said.

He slapped the ragged man on the shoulder, and the Bum's countenance darkened.

"Is it standard for you Herald Class guys to always dress in rags?"

The Tramp ignored him as the Gent ogled a beautiful coed.

"You can tell your boss this rock is not worth taking from my boss. Did you guys ever win one of these walk throughs?"

"You are pathetic when it's your turn to choose who we monitor. You took me to those burdened under your influences as usual," the bum said.

"How long are the days in your week, and how many billions are more than handfuls for you guys? Your office invented Free Will and sat back while humans corrupted it for evil more often than seconds in an eon."

His nemesis scoffed.

"Anyway, we played no part in the drama whose curtain fell here. We're not to blame for how parents raise their children," the Gent said.

"You invaded their father's head and slept in their mother's bed long before their births."

"Blame it on professionalism," the Gent said.

"I will acquaint you with some of our people on our next walk through."

The Distinguished Gent laughed.

"He planned to pad the pool again as he did with Job back in the day."

"Hope and faith are alive and well, and Job was not a fix," the sad bum said.

"Go save a life or something. Oh, you can't. It's not your mission."

"If they taught Job's crap in schools, four-year-olds would stone teachers and call Job a wuss," the Gent continued.

"Unfortunate, indeed."

The Distinguished Gent winked at the beautiful coed and nodded toward his Bentley. She bobbed her head and smiled yes.

The Distinguished Gent slapped the Bum on the shoulder.

"Go home. Your boss backs dead horses for a living."

"How did you figure?" the bum asked.

"You people cannot live down the blot slavery left in the throne room, nor the Jim Crow era that followed. You worked for an all-powerful office, and you should have done something."

He opened the Bentley door for the coed and winked.

"The Lord moves in mysterious ways went blank years before Roman wagon wheels went out of style. Or was it eight track tapes? So don't go there," the Gent said.

The Sad Bum turned away and shuffled off, the gloom deepening on his face.

"Did we waste Free Will on humans? I only worked in the office. It's not for me to answer or even dwell upon."

He glanced back once and continued up the road.

The End

Did you love *The King David Syndrome*? Then you should read *The Legend Of Hallie Elain THompson And The Demon Of Moreland Hill*[1] by Ormine Thompson!

Spanning 306 pages, this gripping supernatural saga traces its origins to the ancient sands of the Middle East, unfolding across centuries before reaching its electrifying climax on a sweltering night in a Negril parking lot, Jamaica. A timeless mystery meets modern revelation—where myth, destiny, magic, and heat collide.

---

1. https://books2read.com/u/3Lvwyw

2. https://books2read.com/u/3Lvwyw